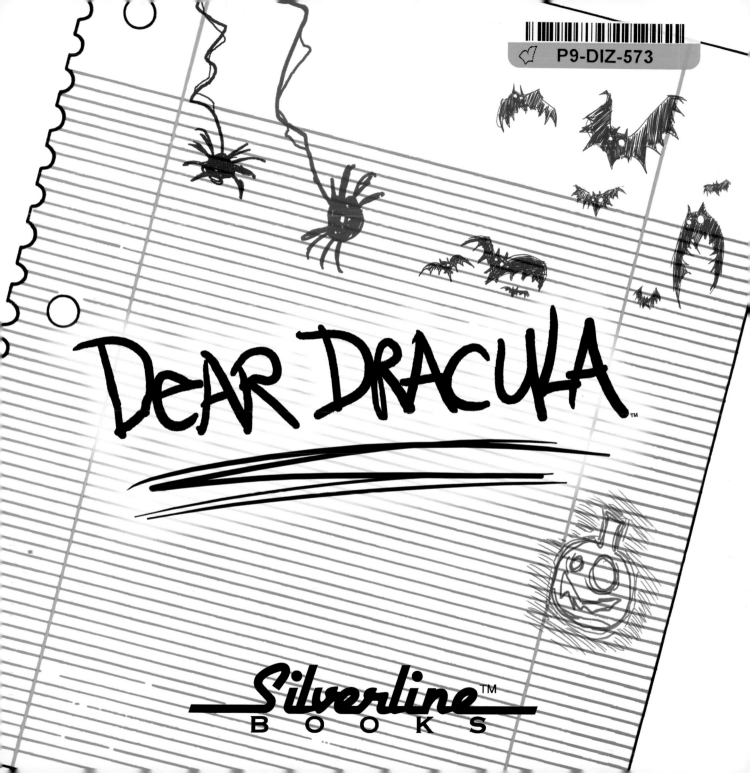

DEAR DRACULA

Silverline™
B O O K S

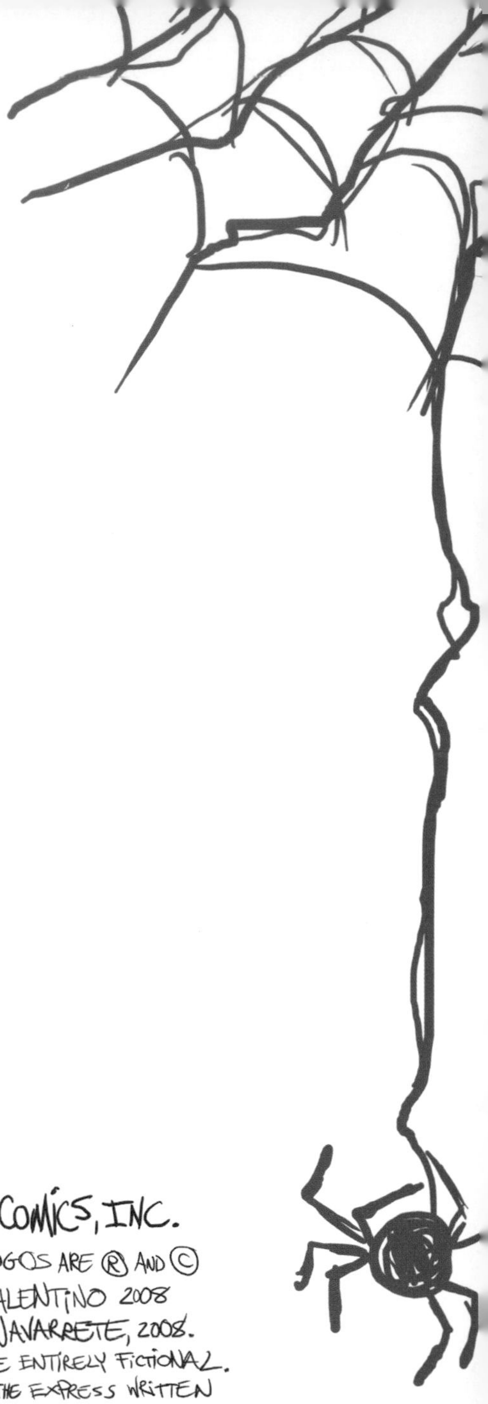

DEAR DRACULA (SEPTEMBER, 2008) IS PUBLISHED BY IMAGE COMICS, INC.
1942 UNIVERSITY AVENUE, SUITE 305, BERKELEY, CA 94704. IMAGE AND ITS LOGOS ARE ® AND ©
2008 IMAGE COMICS, INC. SILVERLINE BOOKS AND ITS LOGOS ARE ™ AND © JIM VALENTINO 2008
DEAR DRACULA AND ITS LOGOS ARE ™ AND © JOSHUA WILLIAMSON AND VICENTE NAVARRETE, 2008.
ALL RIGHTS RESERVED. THE CHARACTERS, EVENTS, AND STORIES IN THIS PUBLICATION ARE ENTIRELY FICTIONAL.
NO PORTION OF THIS BOOK MAY BE REPRODUCED, SAVE FOR PURPOSES OF REVIEW, WITHOUT THE EXPRESS WRITTEN
CONSENT OF MR. WILLIAMSON AND MR. NAVARRETE.   PRINTED IN CANADA.

WRITTEN BY JOSHUA WILLIAMSON

ILLUSTRATED BY Vicente "Vinny" NAVARRETE

EDITED BY KRISTEN SIMON

PUBLISHED BY JIM VALENTINO

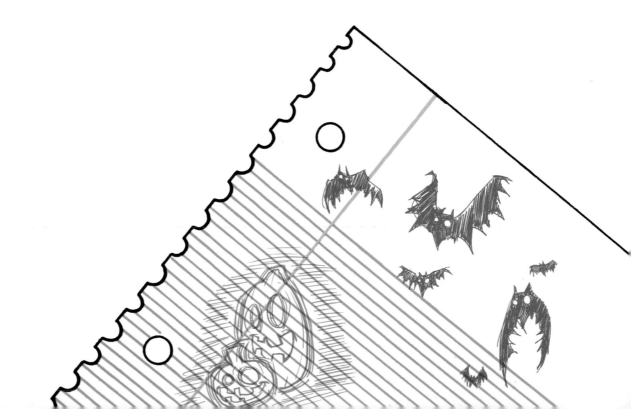

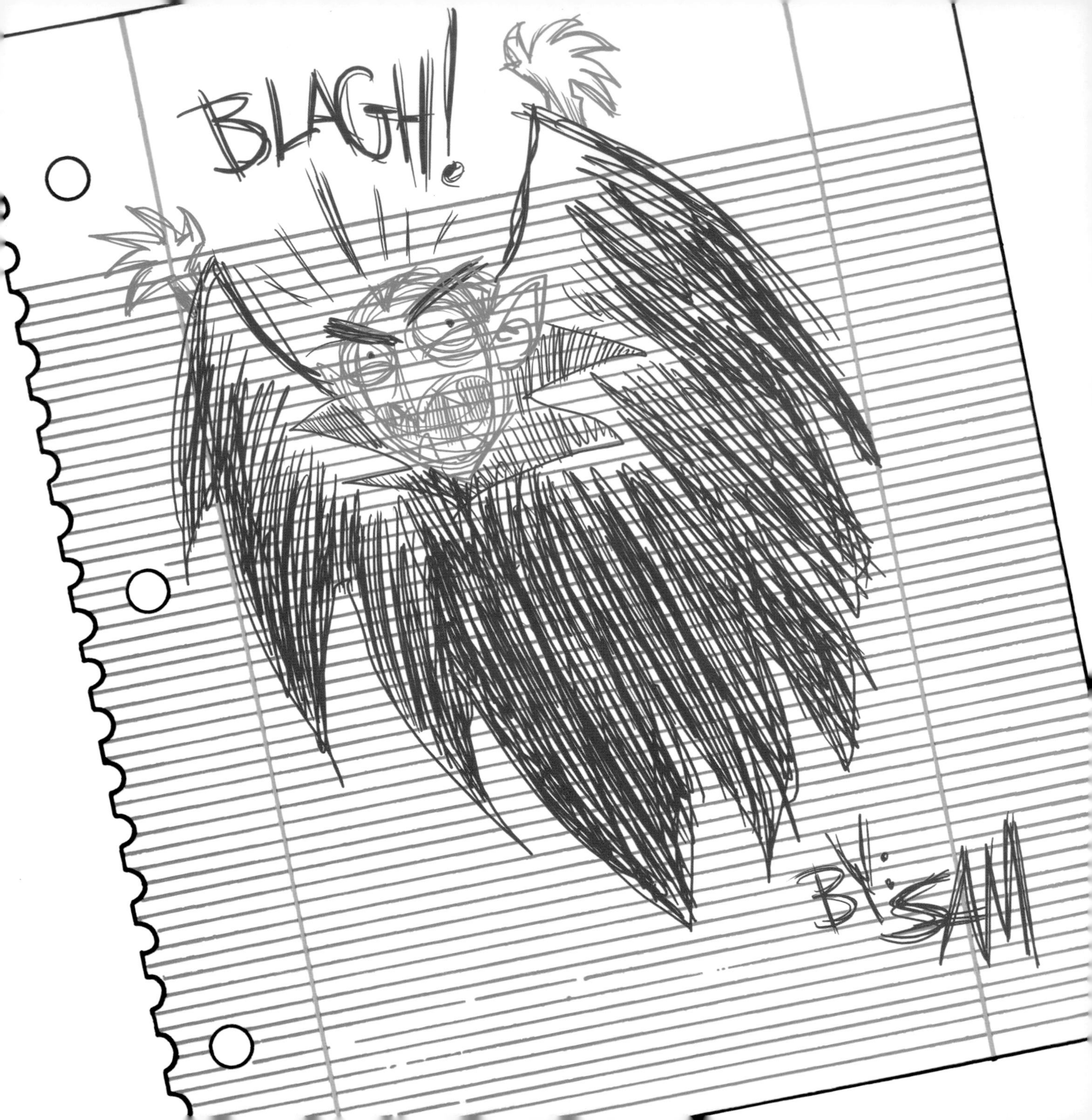
BLAGH!
BY: SAM

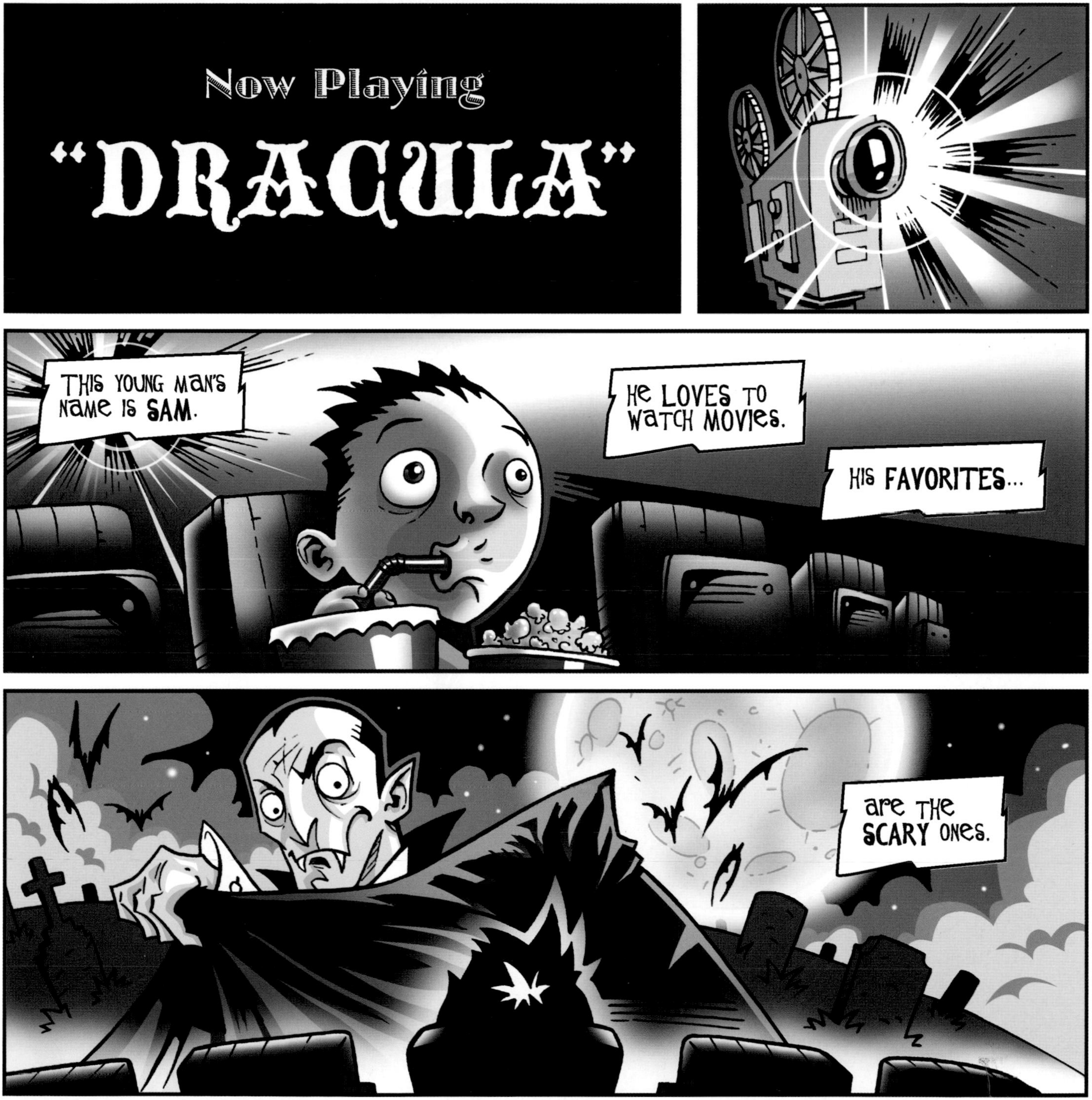
Now Playing
"DRACULA"
THIS YOUNG MAN'S NAME IS SAM.
HE LOVES TO WATCH MOVIES.
HIS FAVORITES...
are THE SCARY ONES.

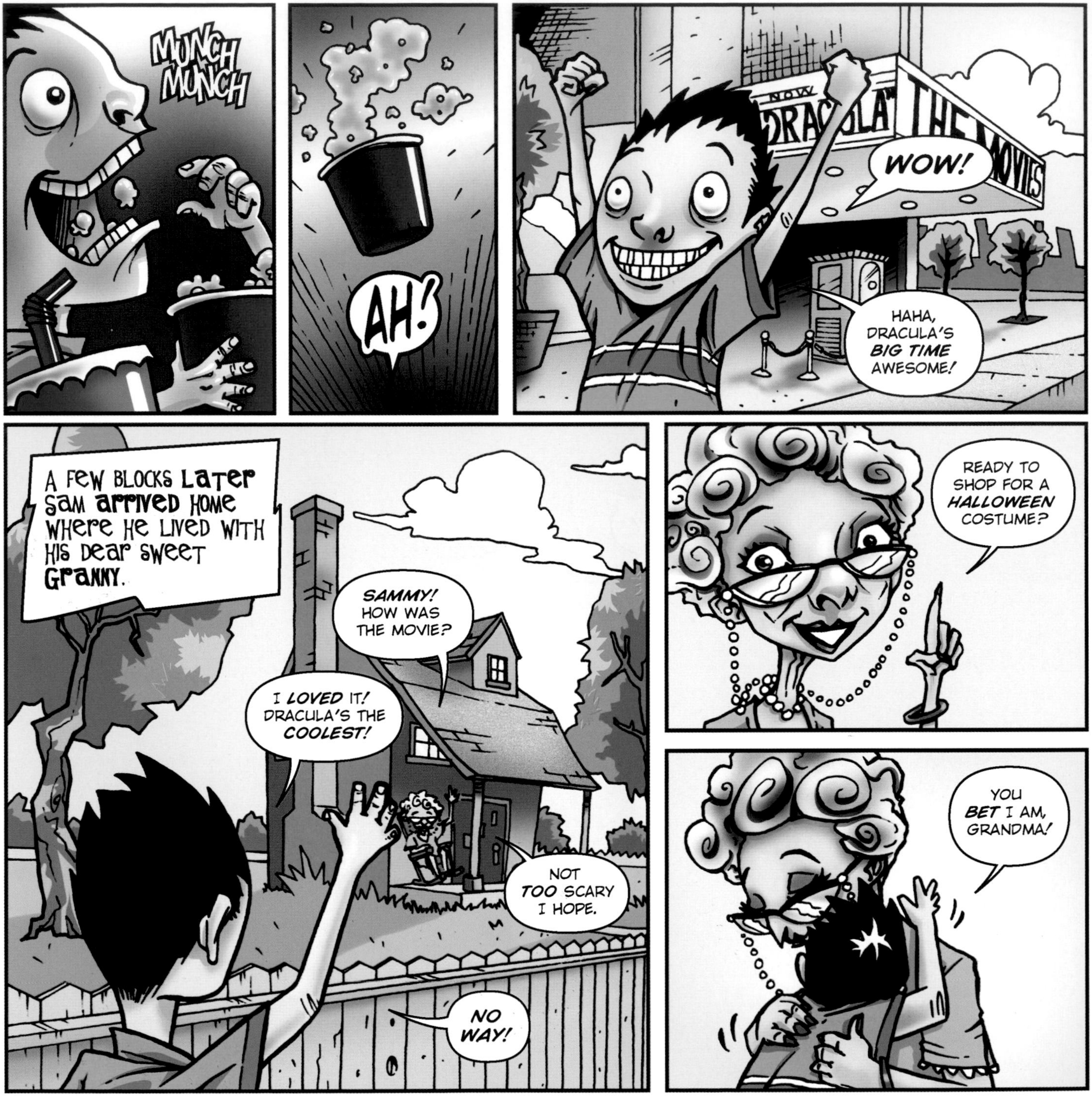
MUNCH MUNCH
AH!
NOW DRACULA THE MOVIES
WOW!
HAHA, DRACULA'S BIG TIME AWESOME!
A FEW BLOCKS LATER SAM ARRIVED HOME WHERE HE LIVED WITH HIS DEAR SWEET GRANNY.
SAMMY! HOW WAS THE MOVIE?
I LOVED IT! DRACULA'S THE COOLEST!
NOT TOO SCARY I HOPE.
NO WAY!
READY TO SHOP FOR A HALLOWEEN COSTUME?
YOU BET I AM, GRANDMA!

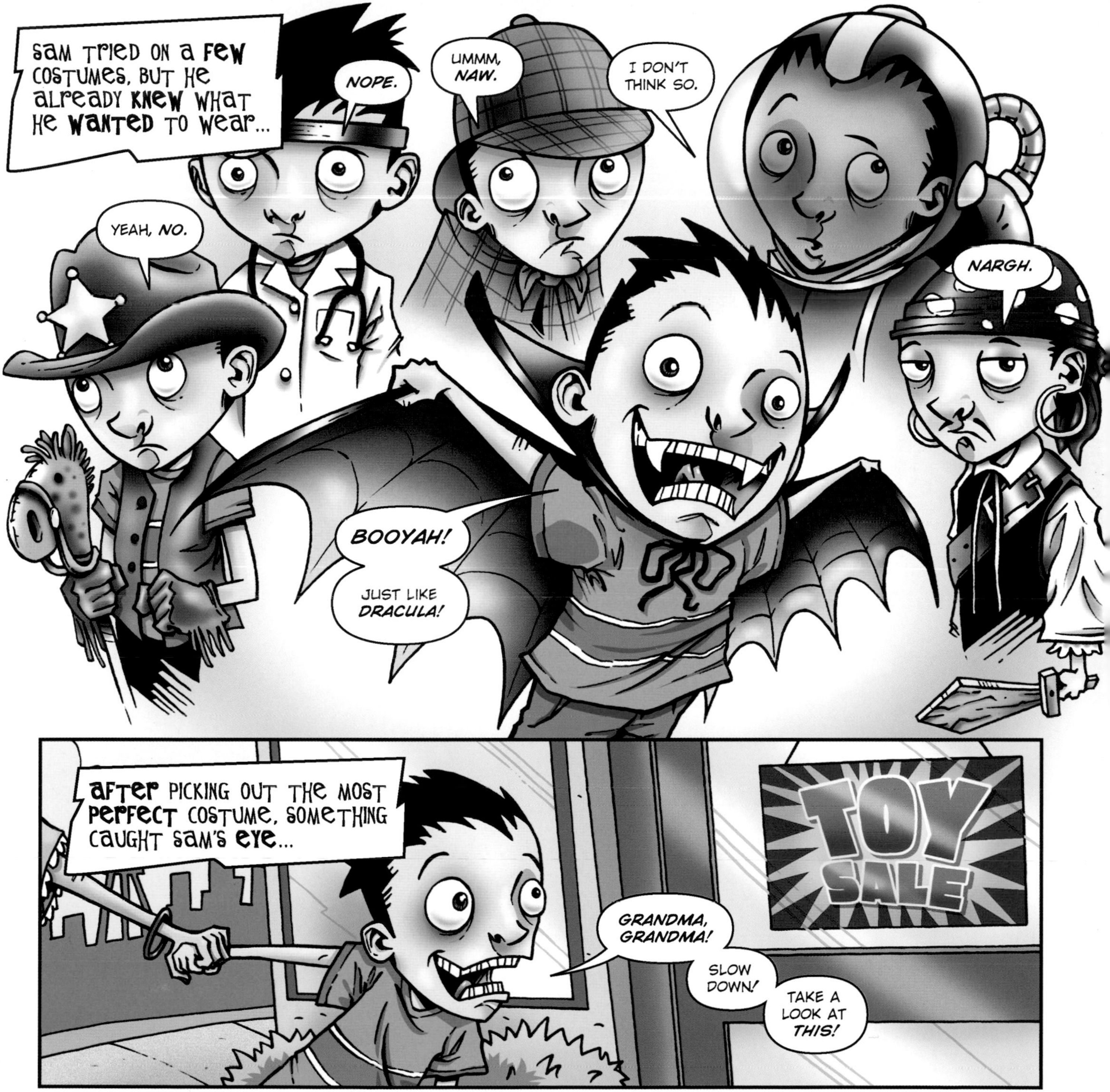
SAM TRIED ON A FEW COSTUMES, BUT HE ALREADY KNEW WHAT HE WANTED TO WEAR...
NOPE.
UMMM, NAW.
I DON'T THINK SO.
YEAH, NO.
NARGH.
BOOYAH!
JUST LIKE DRACULA!
AFTER PICKING OUT THE MOST PERFECT COSTUME, SOMETHING CAUGHT SAM'S EYE...
TOY SALE
GRANDMA, GRANDMA!
SLOW DOWN!
TAKE A LOOK AT THIS!

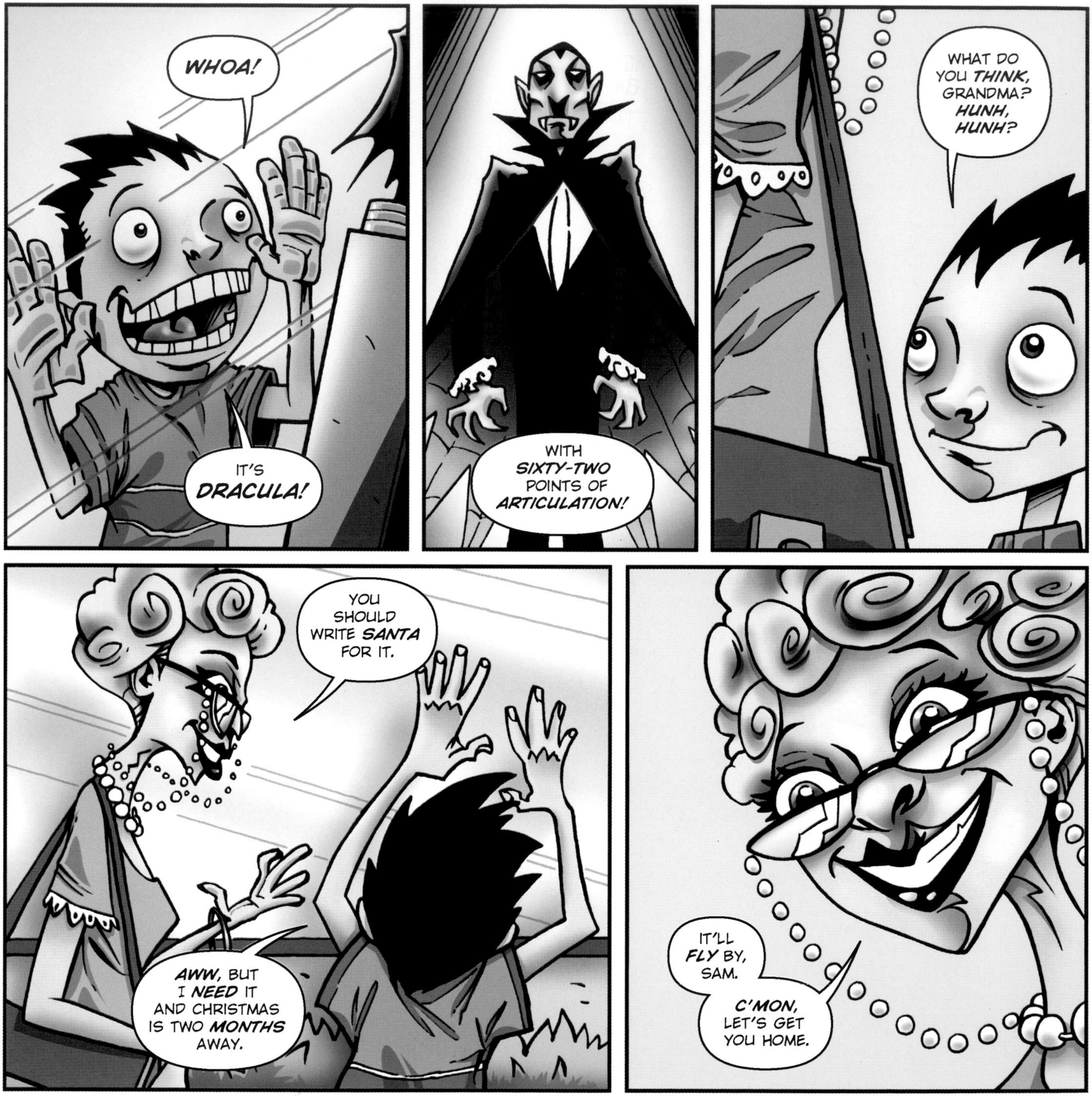
WHOA!
IT'S DRACULA!
WITH SIXTY-TWO POINTS OF ARTICULATION!
WHAT DO YOU THINK, GRANDMA? HUNH, HUNH?
YOU SHOULD WRITE SANTA FOR IT.
AWW, BUT I NEED IT AND CHRISTMAS IS TWO MONTHS AWAY.
IT'LL FLY BY, SAM.
C'MON, LET'S GET YOU HOME.

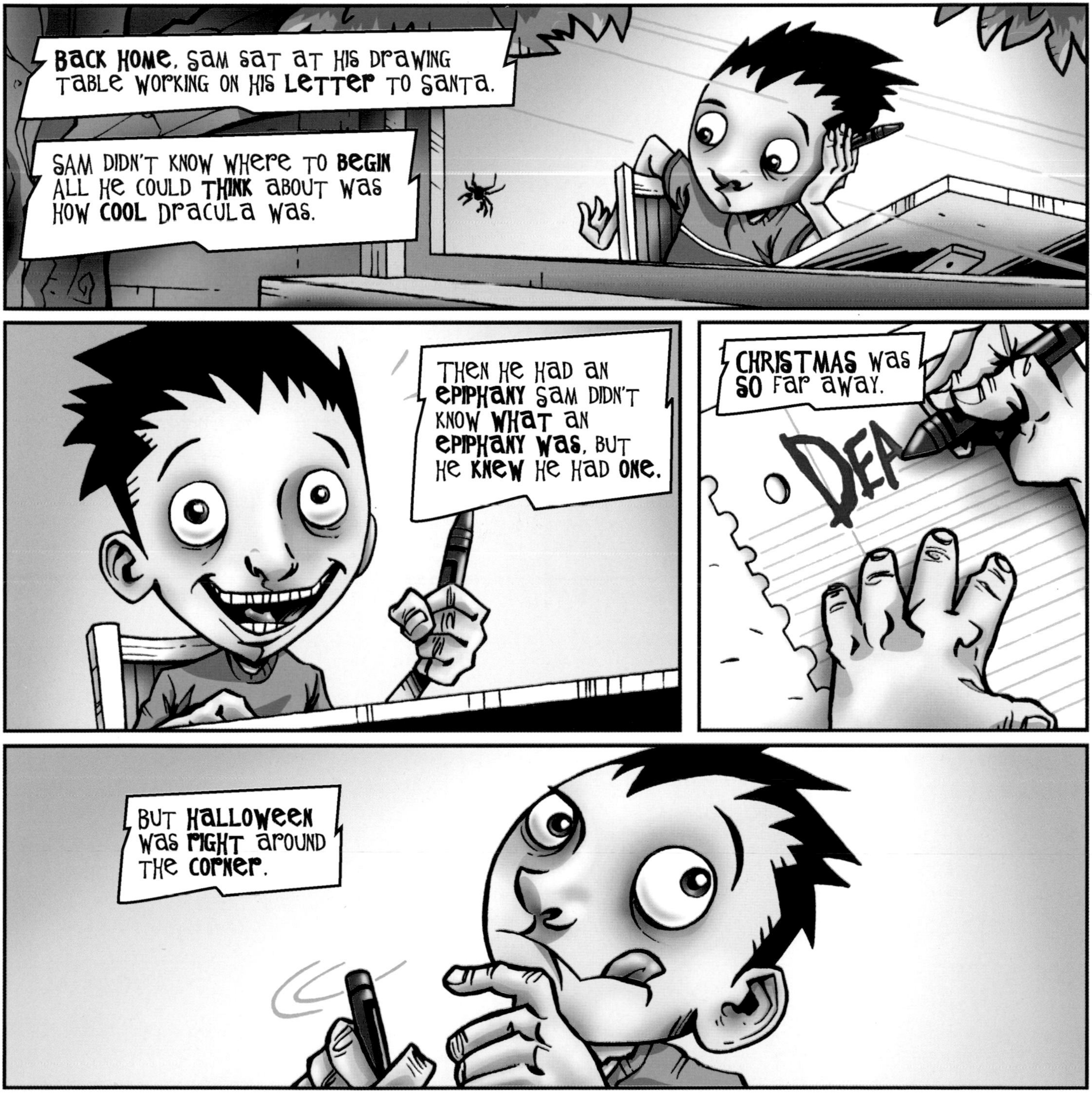
BACK HOME, SAM SAT AT HIS DRAWING TABLE WORKING ON HIS LETTER TO SANTA.
SAM DIDN'T KNOW WHERE TO BEGIN ALL HE COULD THINK ABOUT WAS HOW COOL DRACULA WAS.
THEN HE HAD AN EPIPHANY SAM DIDN'T KNOW WHAT AN EPIPHANY WAS, BUT HE KNEW HE HAD ONE.
CHRISTMAS WAS SO FAR AWAY.
DEA
BUT HALLOWEEN WAS RIGHT AROUND THE CORNER.

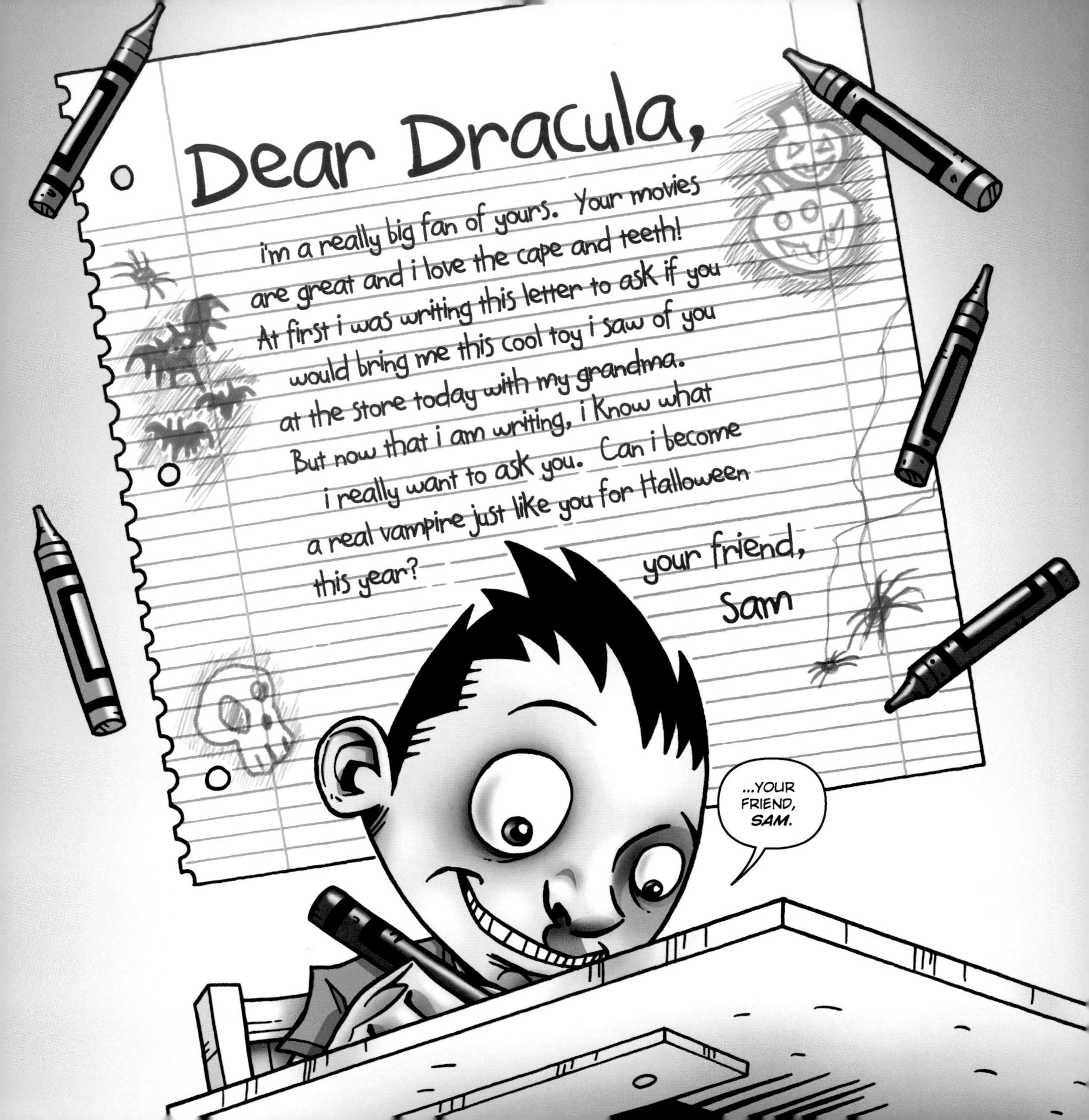
Dear Dracula,
i'm a really big fan of yours. Your movies are great and i love the cape and teeth! At first i was writing this letter to ask if you would bring me this cool toy i saw of you at the store today with my grandma. But now that i am writing, i Know what i really want to ask you. Can i become a real vampire just like you for Halloween this year?
your friend,
Sam
...YOUR FRIEND, SAM.

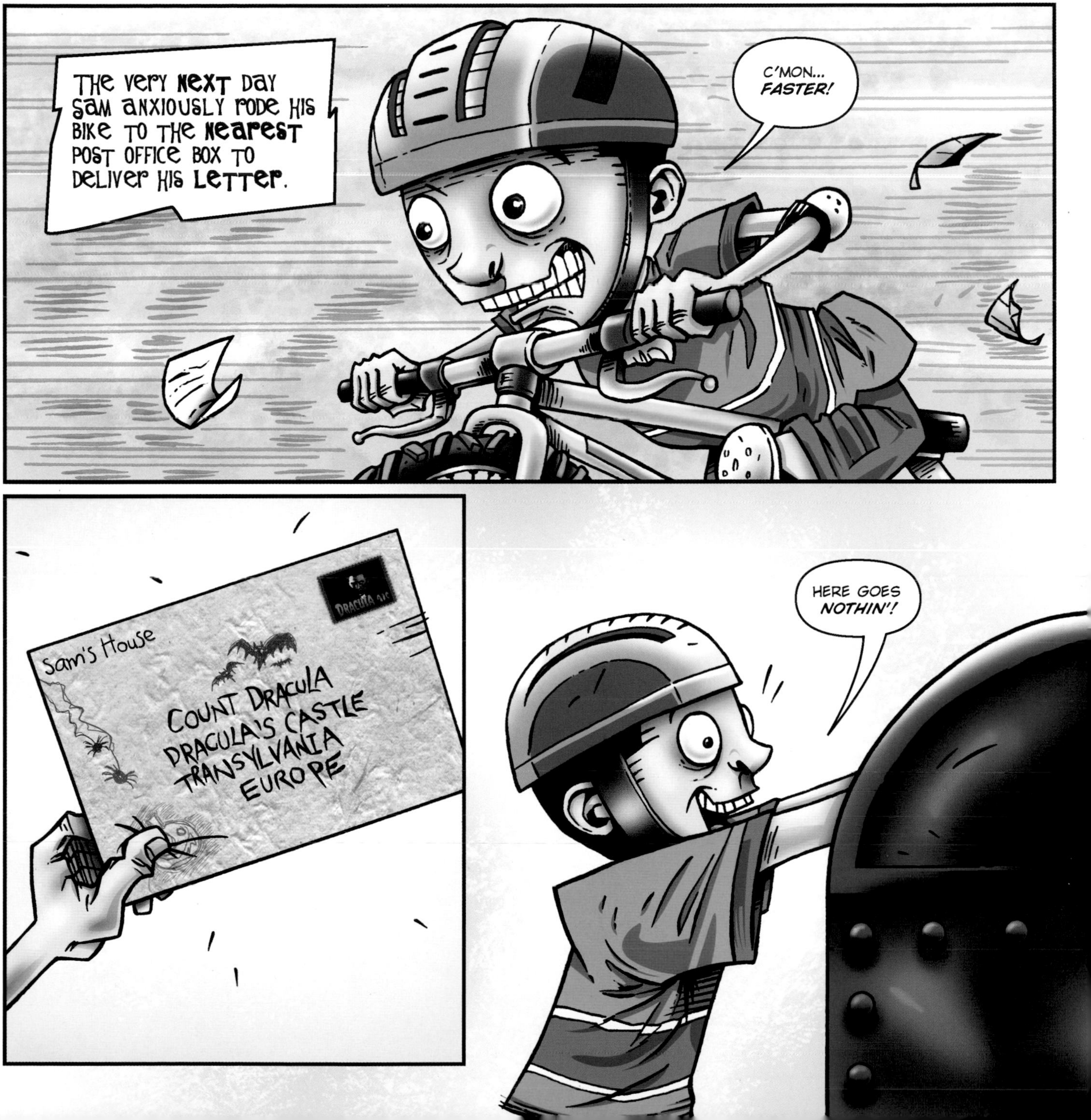
THE VERY NEXT DAY SAM ANXIOUSLY RODE HIS BIKE TO THE NEAREST POST OFFICE BOX TO DELIVER HIS LETTER.
C'MON... FASTER!
Sam's House
COUNT DRACULA
DRACULA'S CASTLE
TRANSYLVANIA
EUROPE
HERE GOES NOTHIN'!

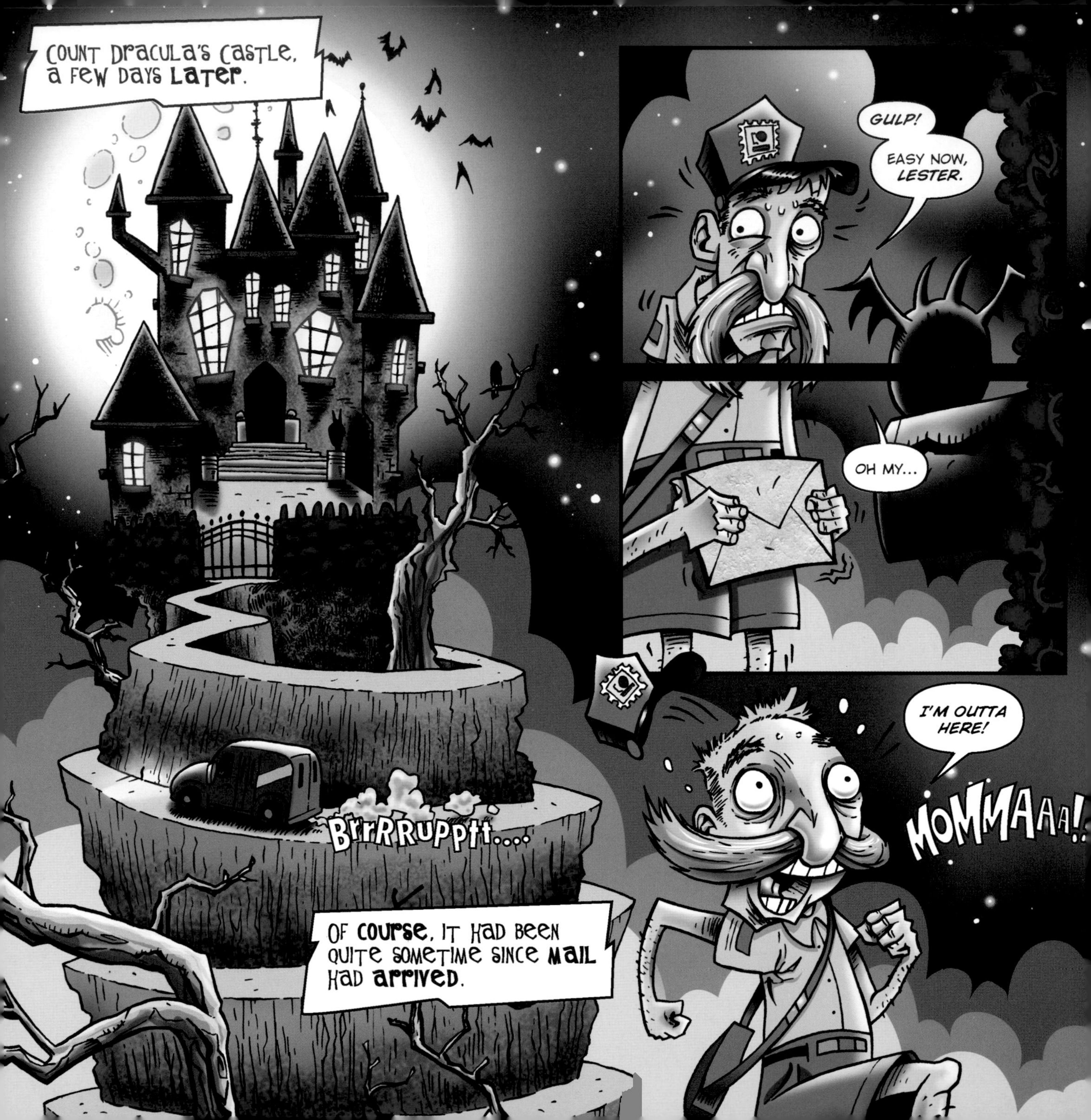
COUNT DRACULA'S CASTLE, A FEW DAYS LATER.
BrrRRUpptt....
OF COURSE, IT HAD BEEN QUITE SOMETIME SINCE MAIL HAD ARRIVED.
GULP!
EASY NOW, LESTER.
OH MY...
I'M OUTTA HERE!
MOMMAAA!!

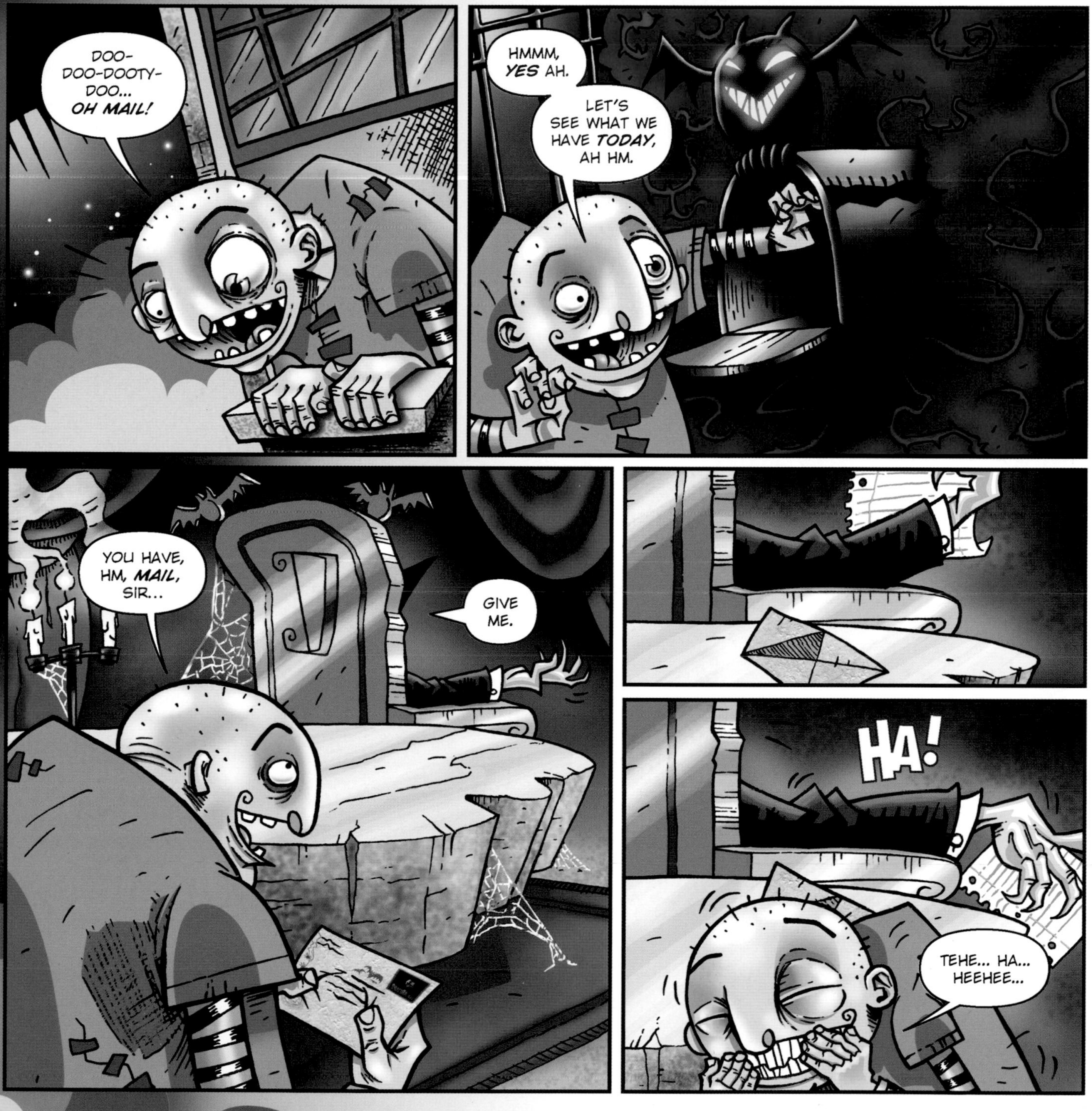

DOO-DOO-DOOTY-DOO... OH MAIL!
HMMM, YES AH.
LET'S SEE WHAT WE HAVE TODAY, AH HM.
YOU HAVE, HM, MAIL, SIR...
GIVE ME.
HA!
TEHE... HA... HEEHEE...

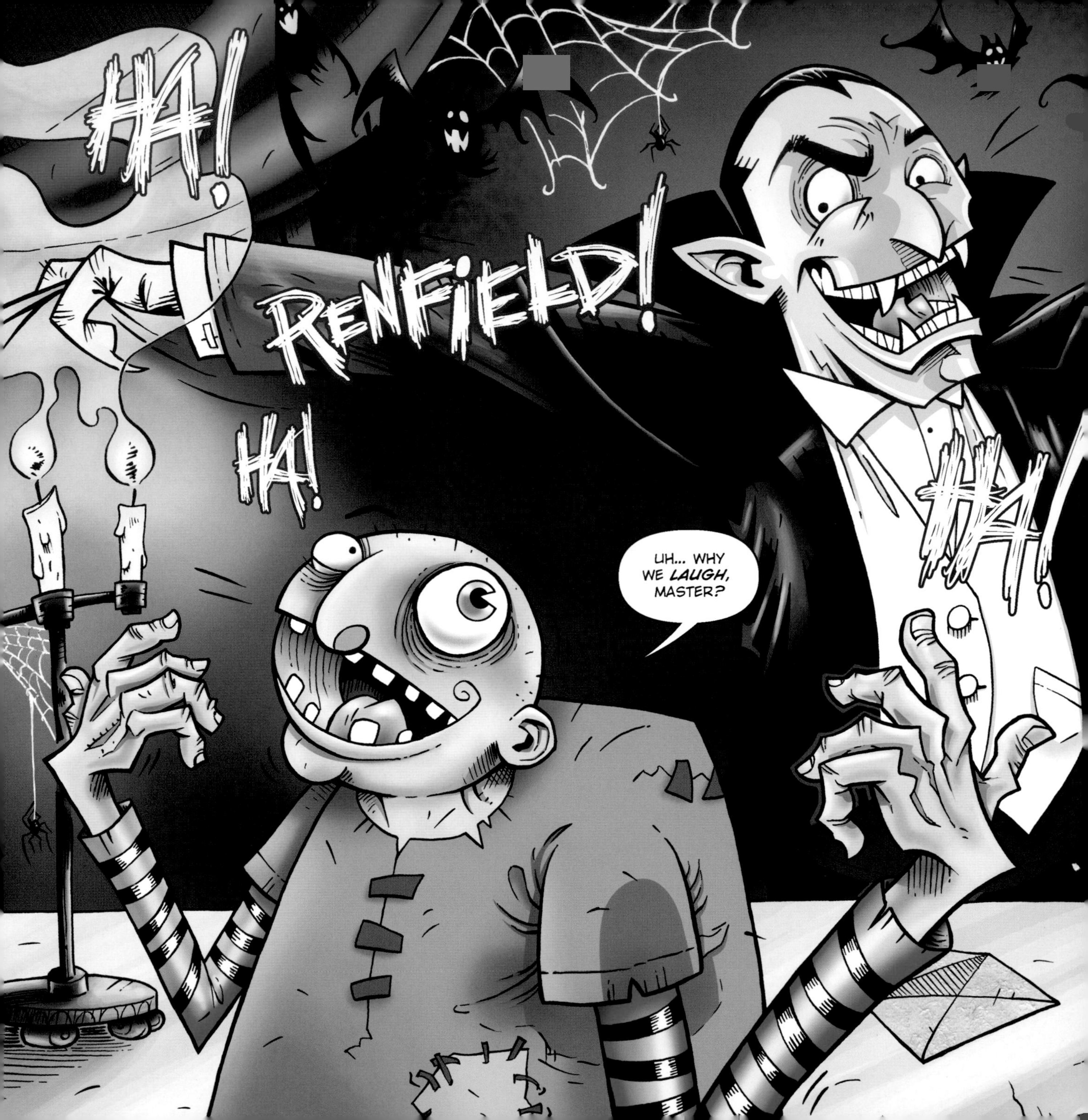
HA!
RENFIELD!
HA!
HA!
UH... WHY WE *LAUGH*, MASTER?

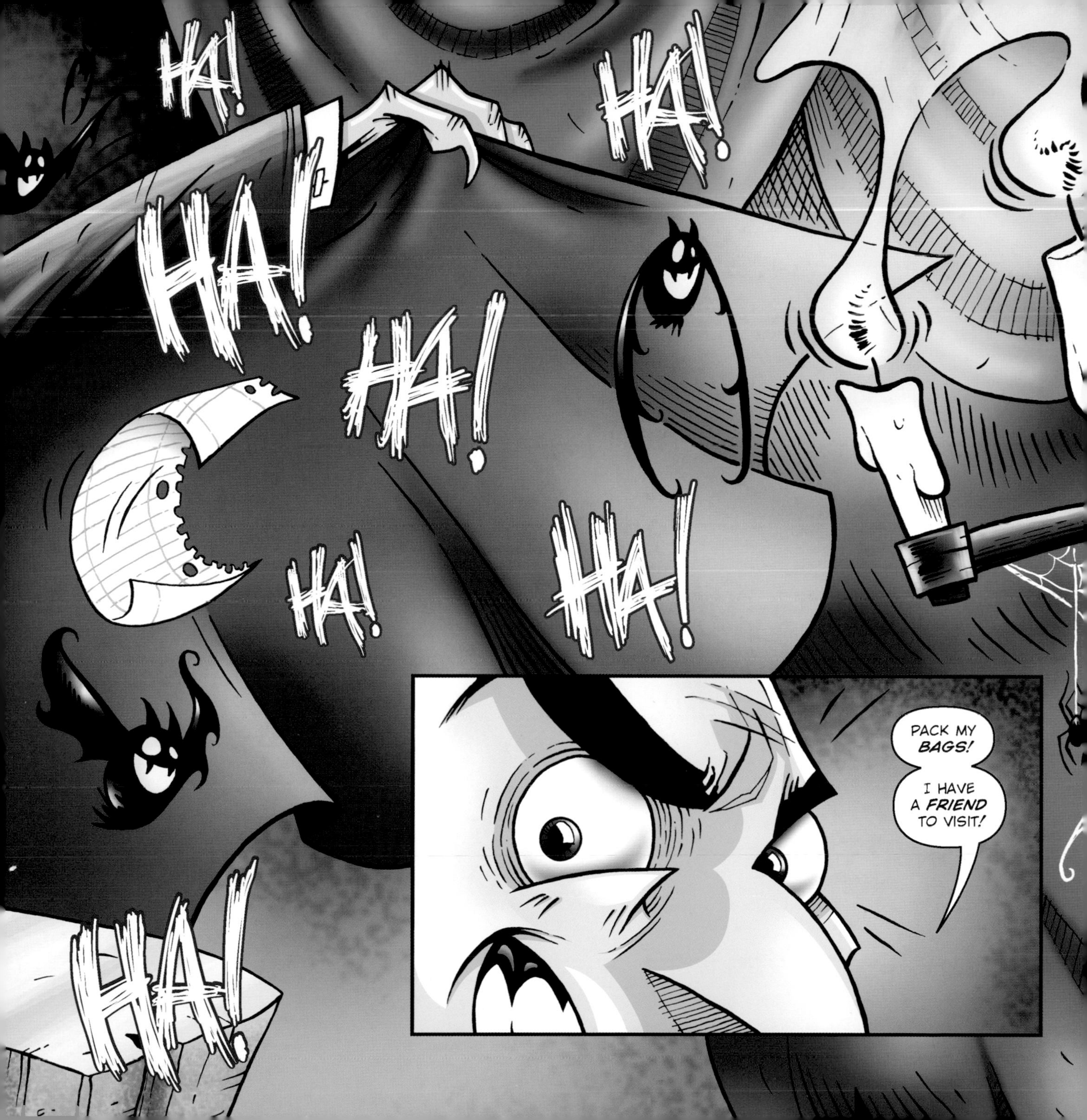
HA!
HA!
HA!
HA!
HA!
HA!
HA!
HA!
PACK MY *BAGS!*
I HAVE A *FRIEND* TO VISIT!

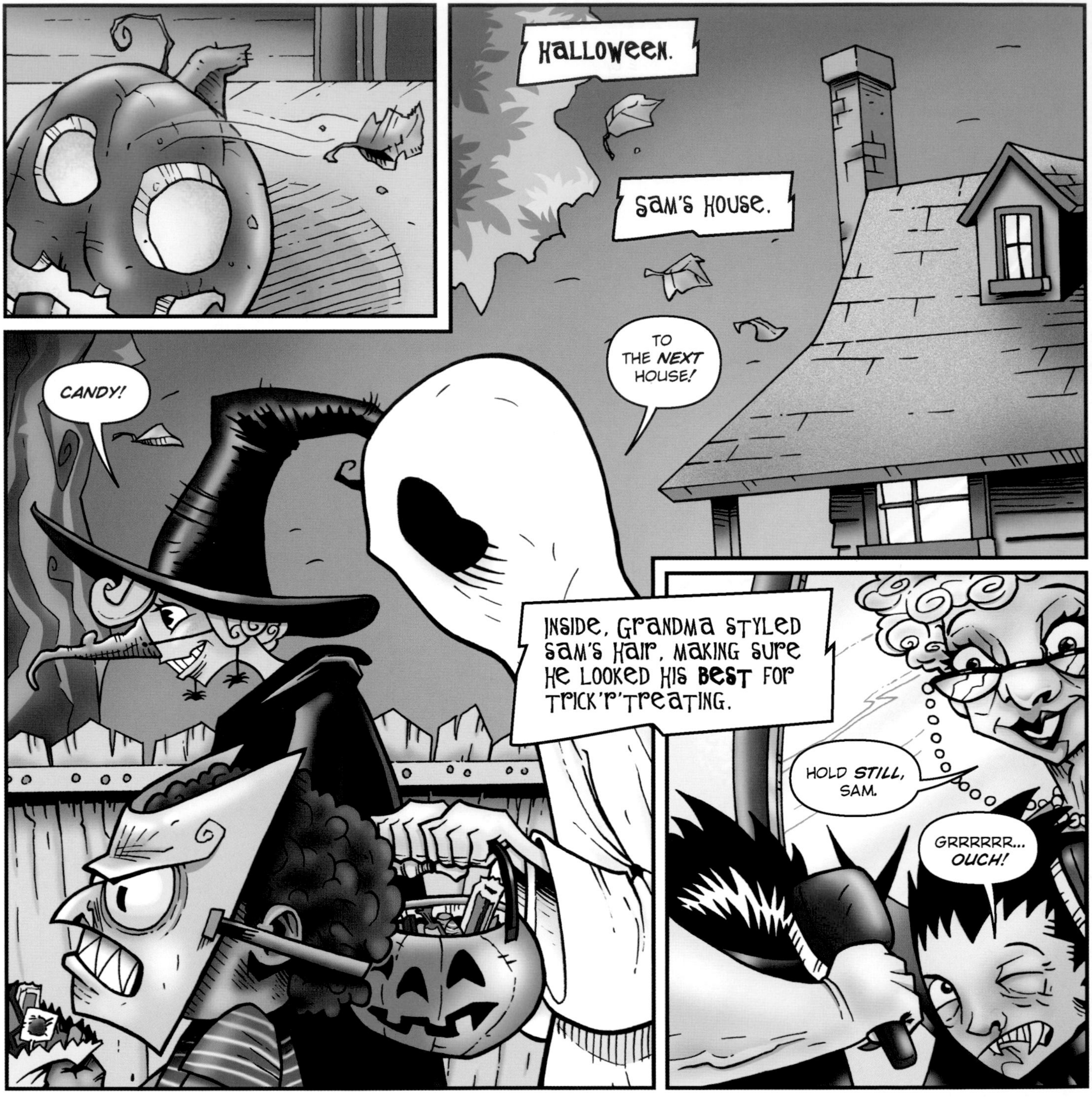
HALLOWEEN.
SAM'S HOUSE.
CANDY!
TO THE NEXT HOUSE!
INSIDE, GRANDMA STYLED SAM'S HAIR, MAKING SURE HE LOOKED HIS BEST FOR TRICK'R'TREATING.
HOLD STILL, SAM.
GRRRRRR... OUCH!

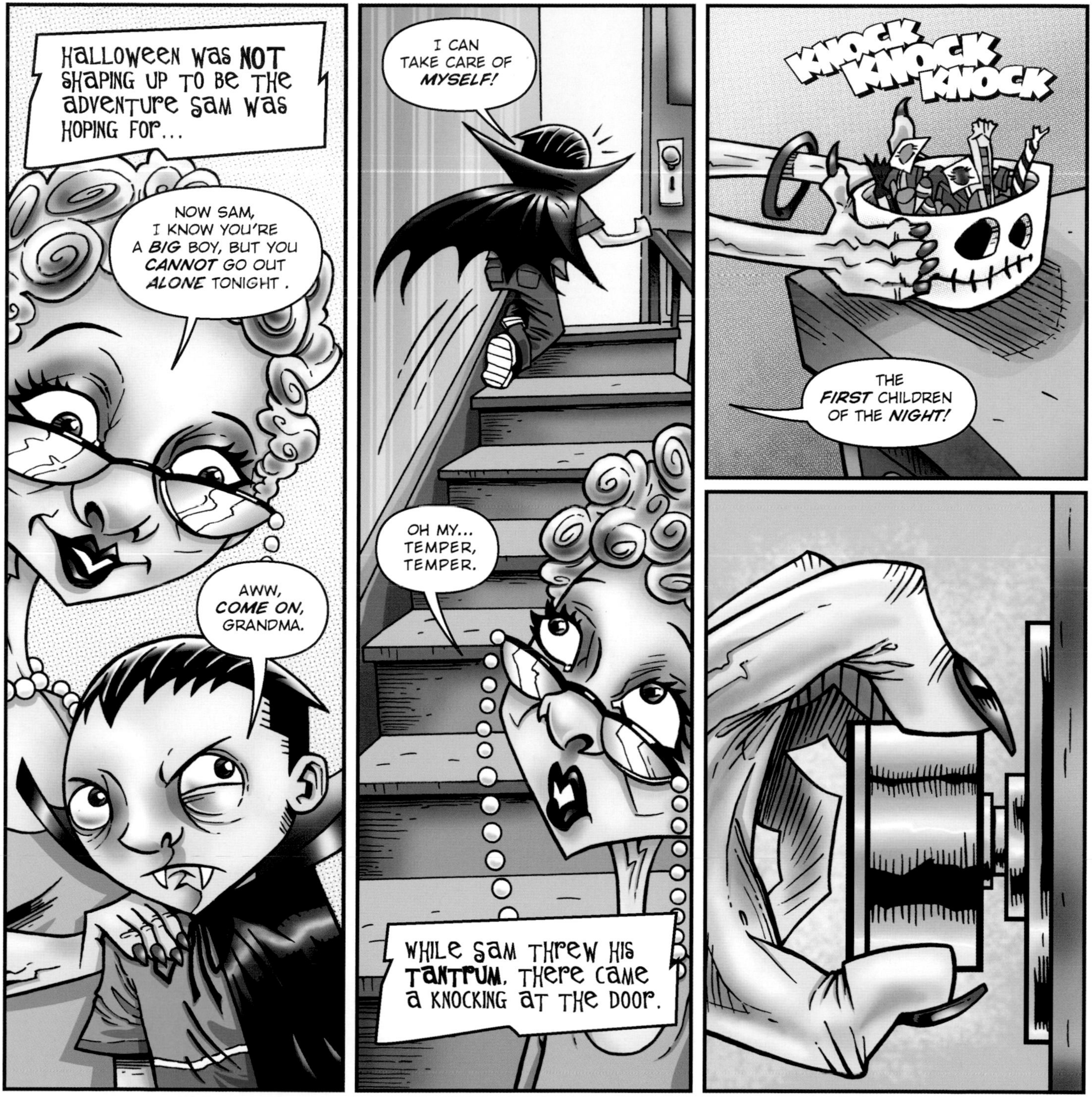
HALLOWEEN WAS NOT SHAPING UP TO BE THE ADVENTURE SAM WAS HOPING FOR...
NOW SAM, I KNOW YOU'RE A BIG BOY, BUT YOU CANNOT GO OUT ALONE TONIGHT.
AWW, COME ON, GRANDMA.
I CAN TAKE CARE OF MYSELF!
OH MY... TEMPER, TEMPER.
WHILE SAM THREW HIS TANTRUM, THERE CAME A KNOCKING AT THE DOOR.
KNOCK KNOCK KNOCK
THE FIRST CHILDREN OF THE NIGHT!

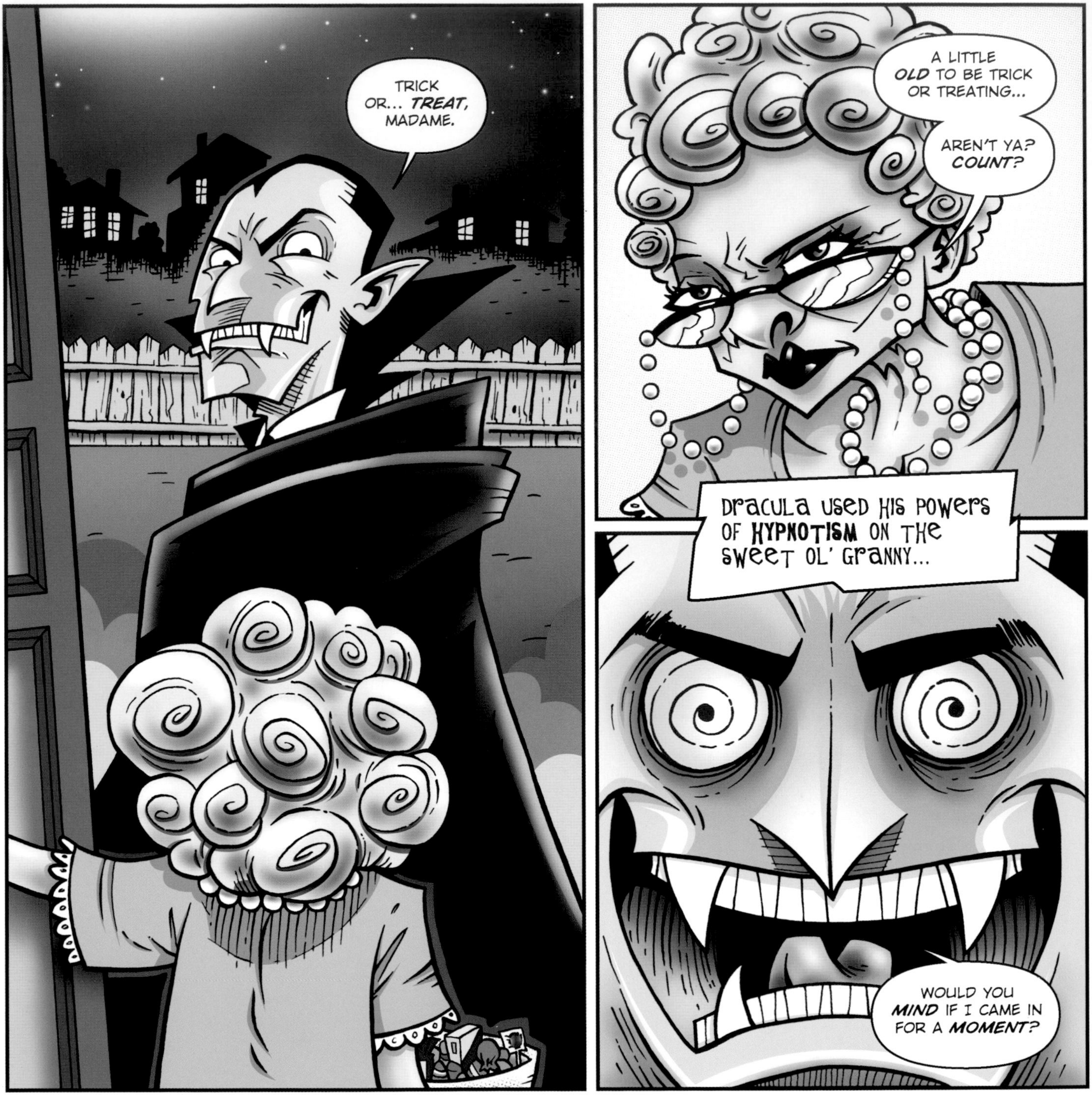
TRICK OR... TREAT, MADAME.
A LITTLE OLD TO BE TRICK OR TREATING...
AREN'T YA? COUNT?
DRACULA USED HIS POWERS OF HYPNOTISM ON THE SWEET OL' GRANNY...
WOULD YOU MIND IF I CAME IN FOR A MOMENT?

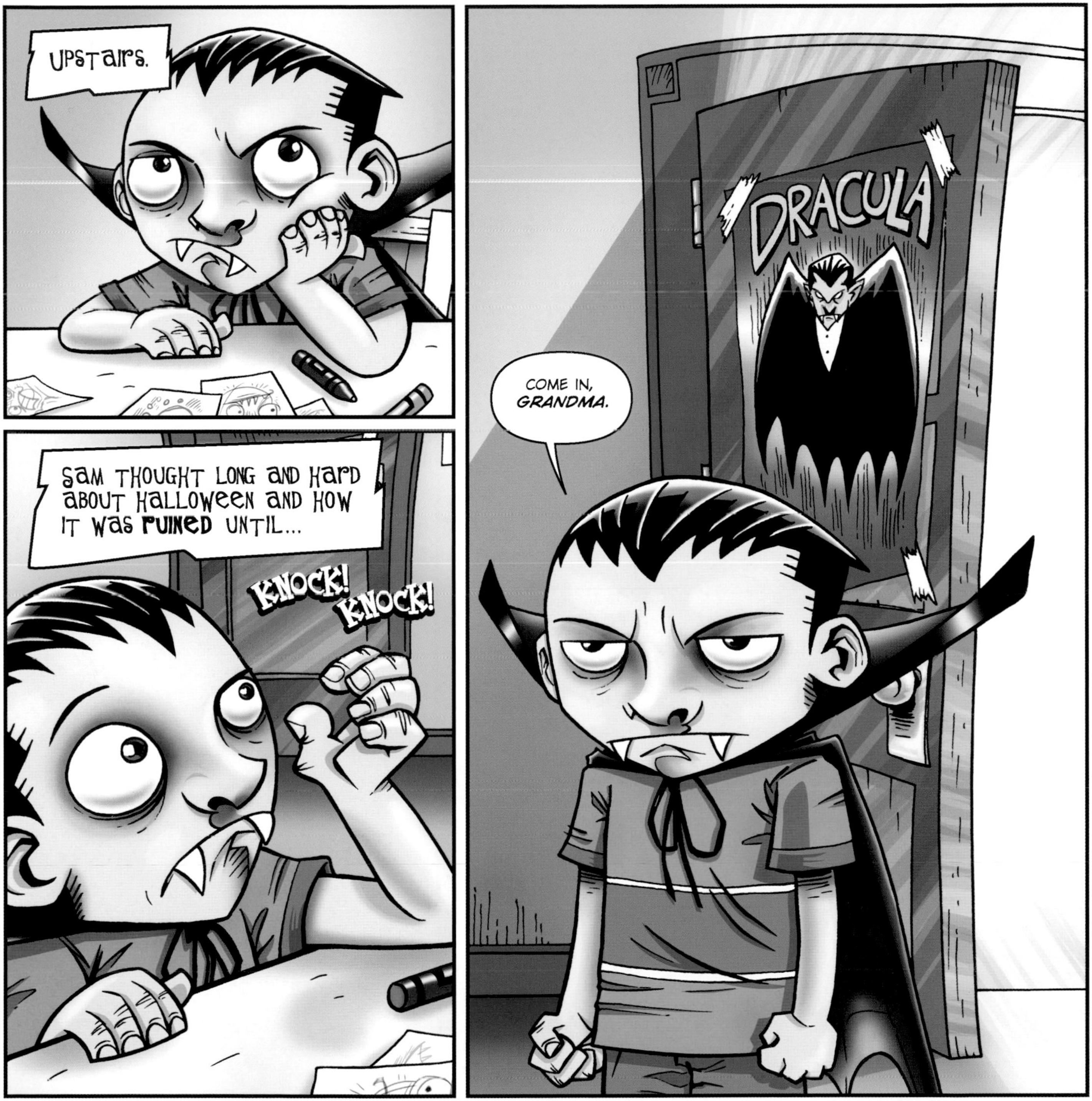
UPSTAIRS.
SAM THOUGHT LONG AND HARD ABOUT HALLOWEEN AND HOW IT WAS **RUINED** UNTIL...
KNOCK! KNOCK!
COME IN, *GRANDMA.*
DRACULA

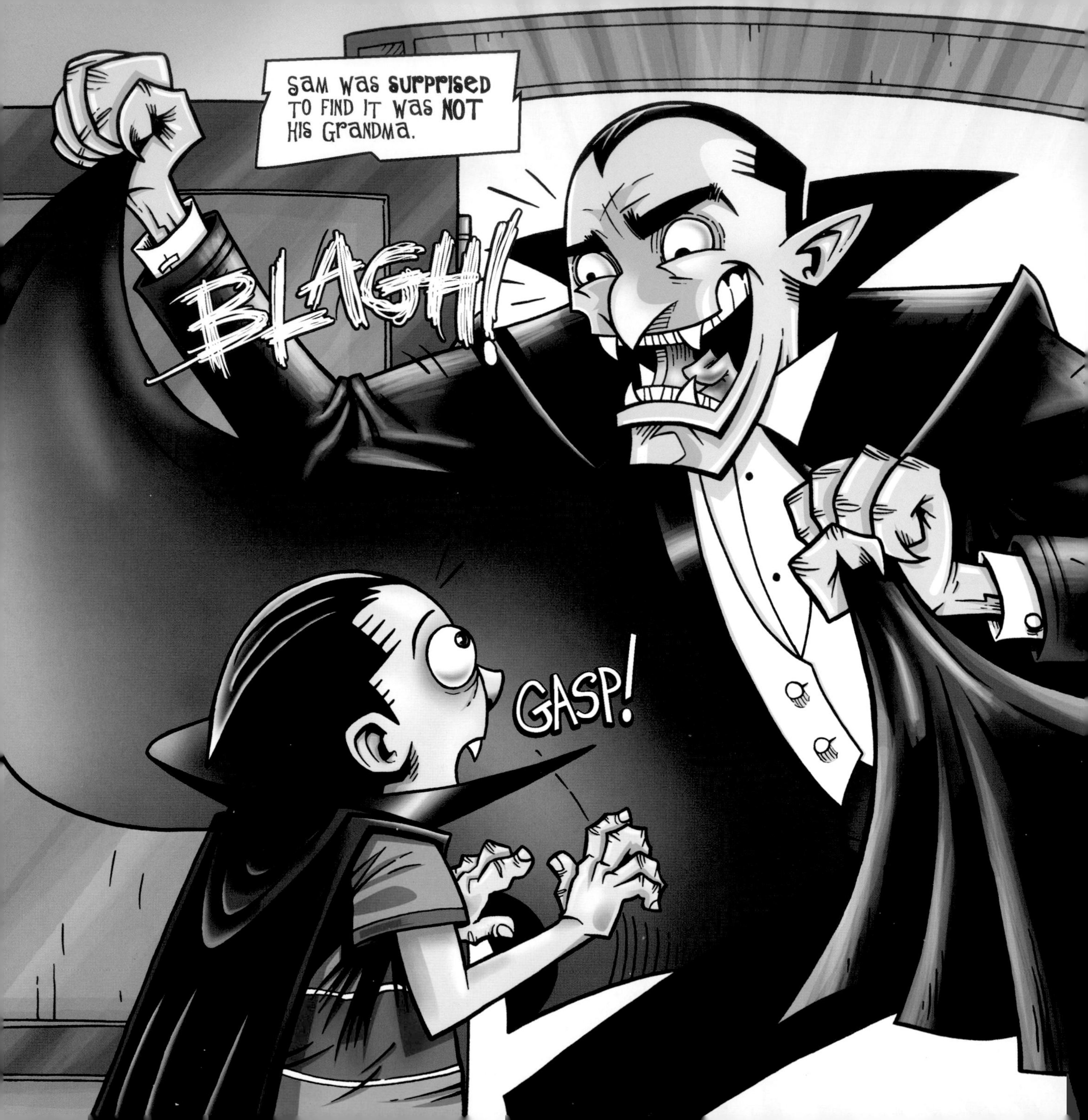
SAM WAS SURPRISED TO FIND IT WAS NOT HIS GRANDMA.
BLAGH!
GASP!

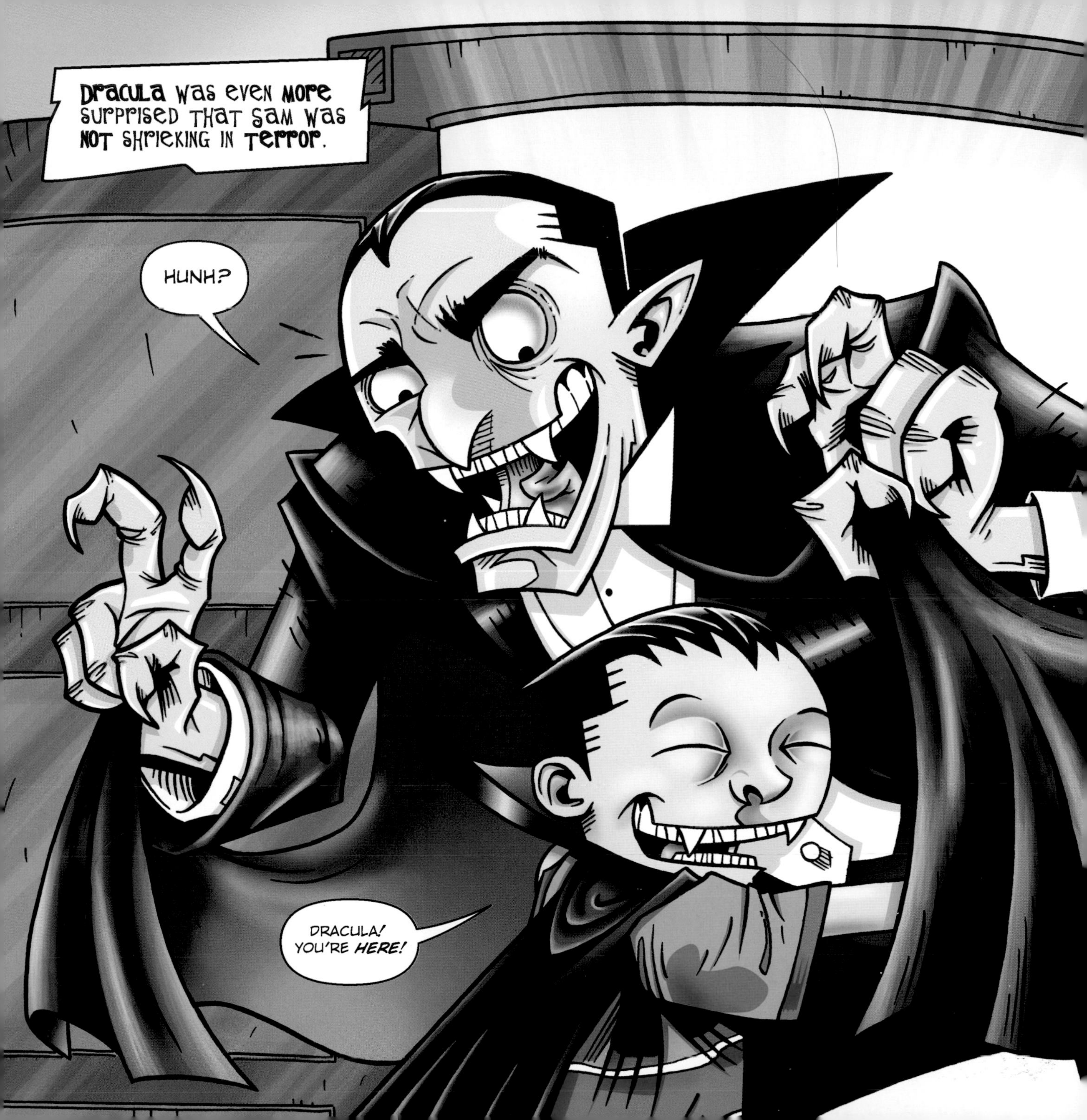
DRACULA WAS EVEN MORE SURPRISED THAT SAM WAS NOT SHRIEKING IN TERROR.
HUNH?
DRACULA! YOU'RE HERE!

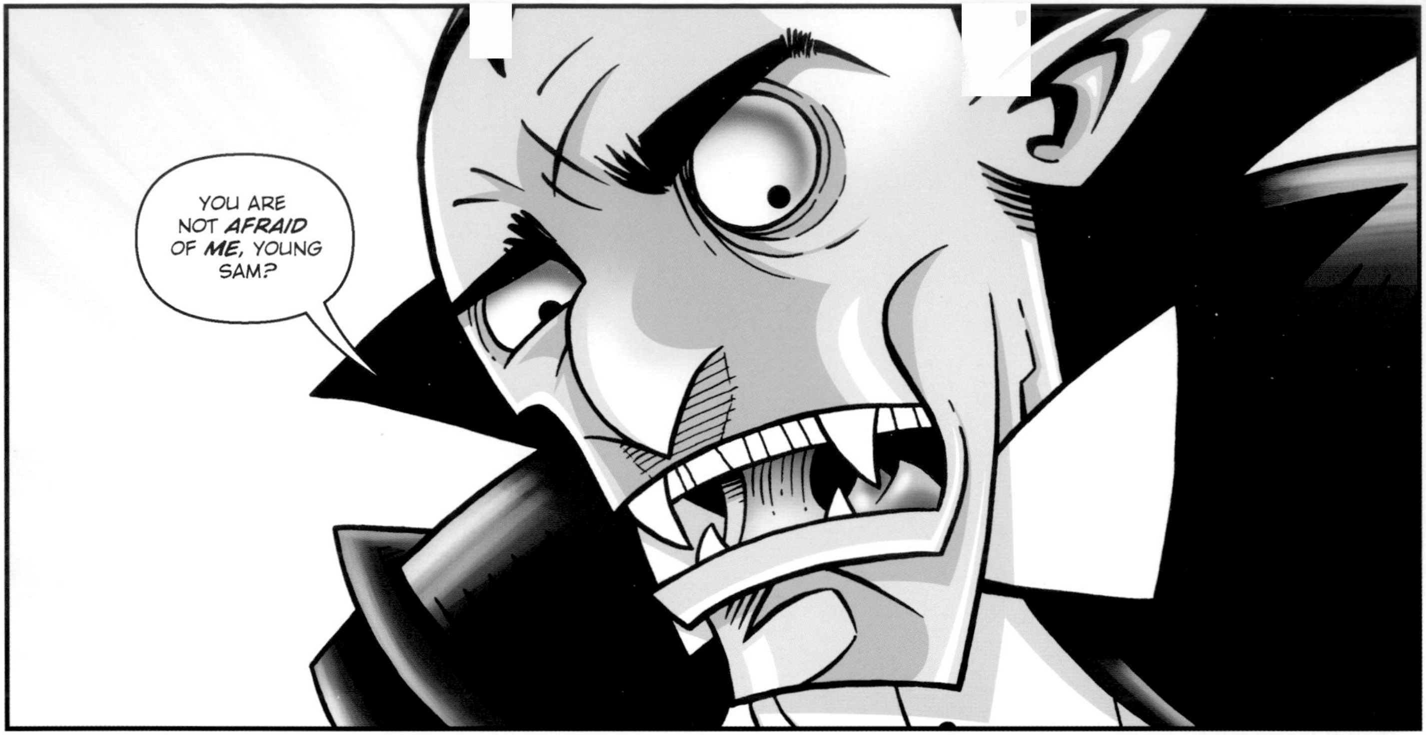
YOU ARE NOT *AFRAID* OF *ME,* YOUNG SAM?

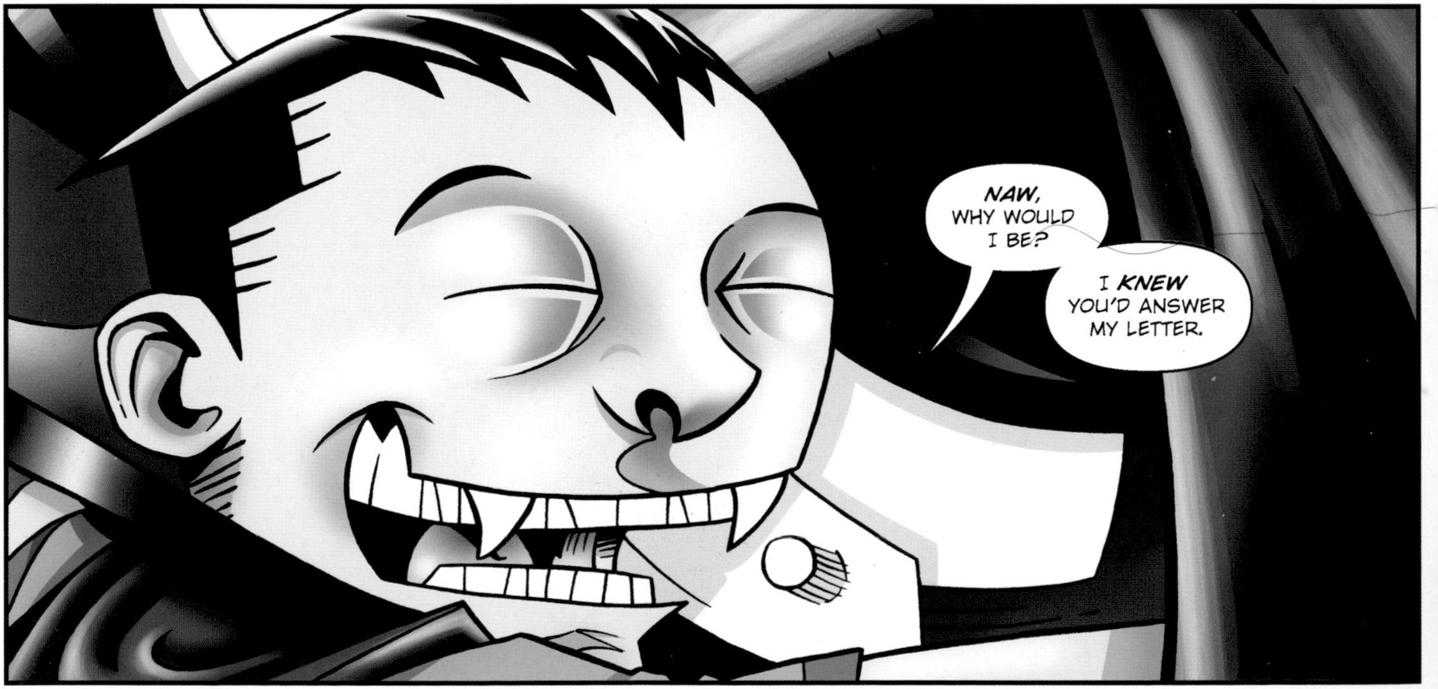
NAW, WHY WOULD I BE?
I *KNEW* YOU'D ANSWER MY LETTER.

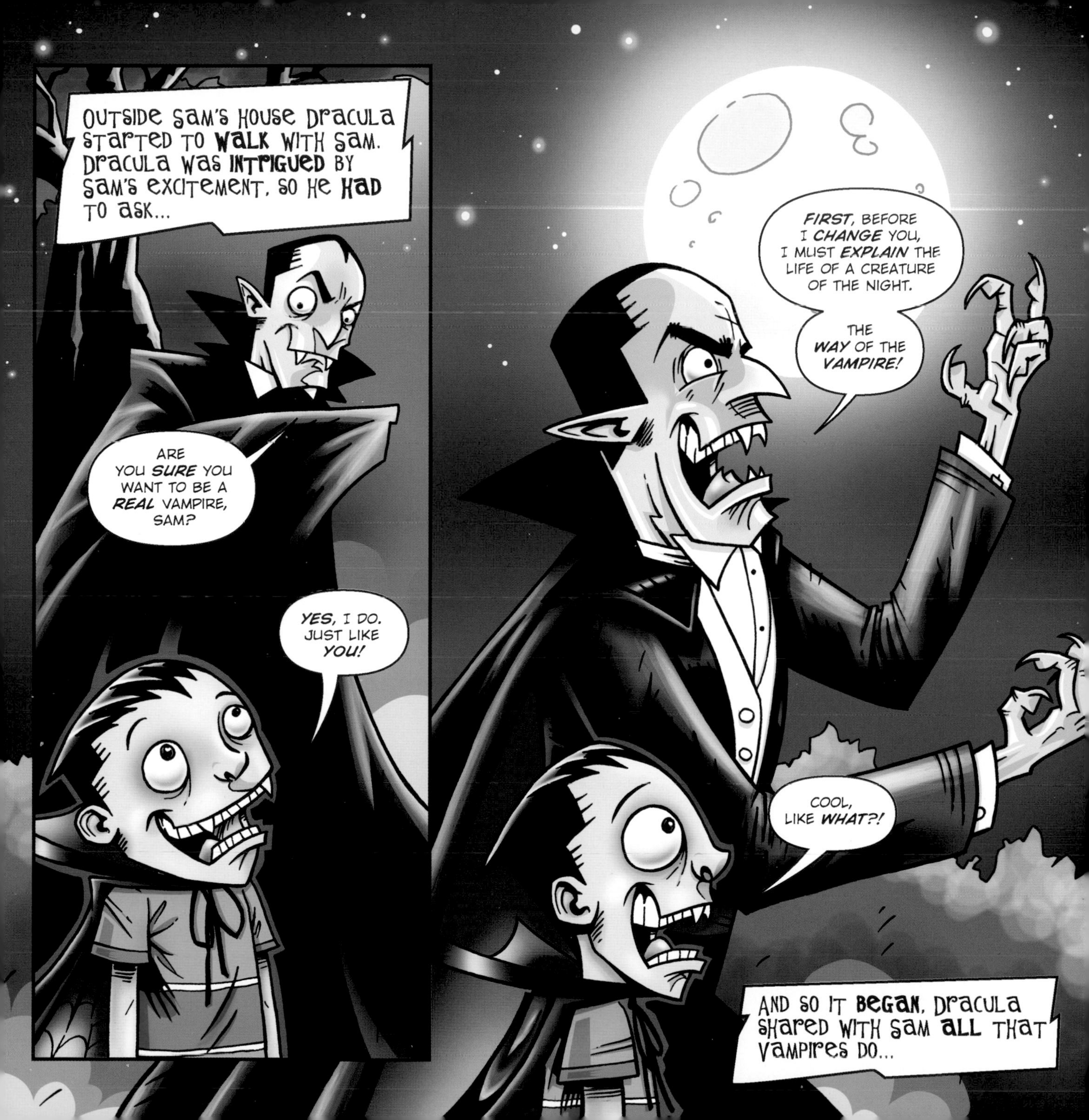

OUTSIDE SAM'S HOUSE DRACULA STARTED TO WALK WITH SAM. DRACULA WAS INTRIGUED BY SAM'S EXCITEMENT, SO HE HAD TO ASK...
ARE YOU SURE YOU WANT TO BE A REAL VAMPIRE, SAM?
YES, I DO. JUST LIKE YOU!
FIRST, BEFORE I CHANGE YOU, I MUST EXPLAIN THE LIFE OF A CREATURE OF THE NIGHT.
THE WAY OF THE VAMPIRE!
COOL, LIKE WHAT?!
AND SO IT BEGAN, DRACULA SHARED WITH SAM ALL THAT VAMPIRES DO...

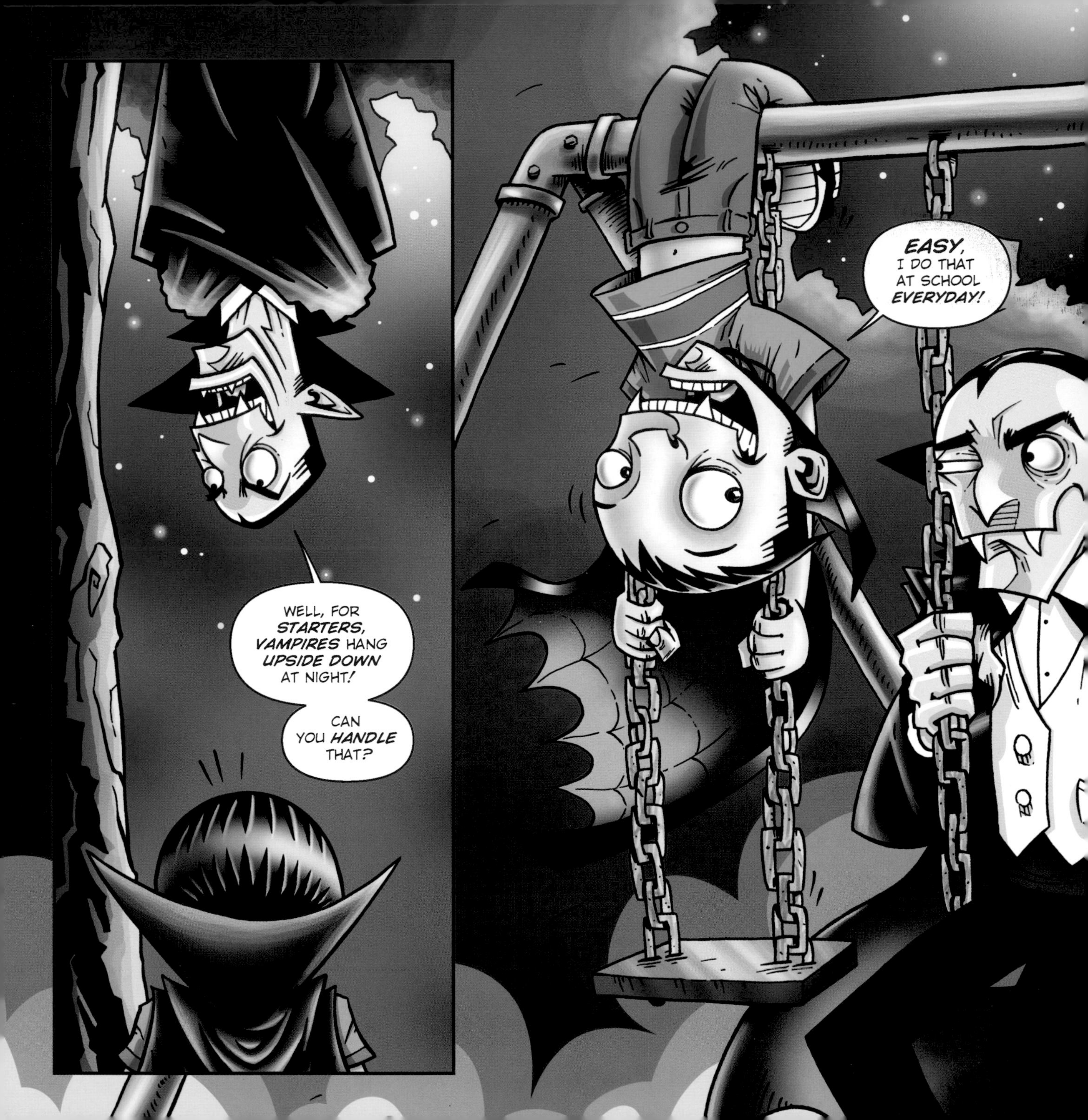
WELL, FOR STARTERS, VAMPIRES HANG UPSIDE DOWN AT NIGHT!
CAN YOU HANDLE THAT?
EASY, I DO THAT AT SCHOOL EVERYDAY!

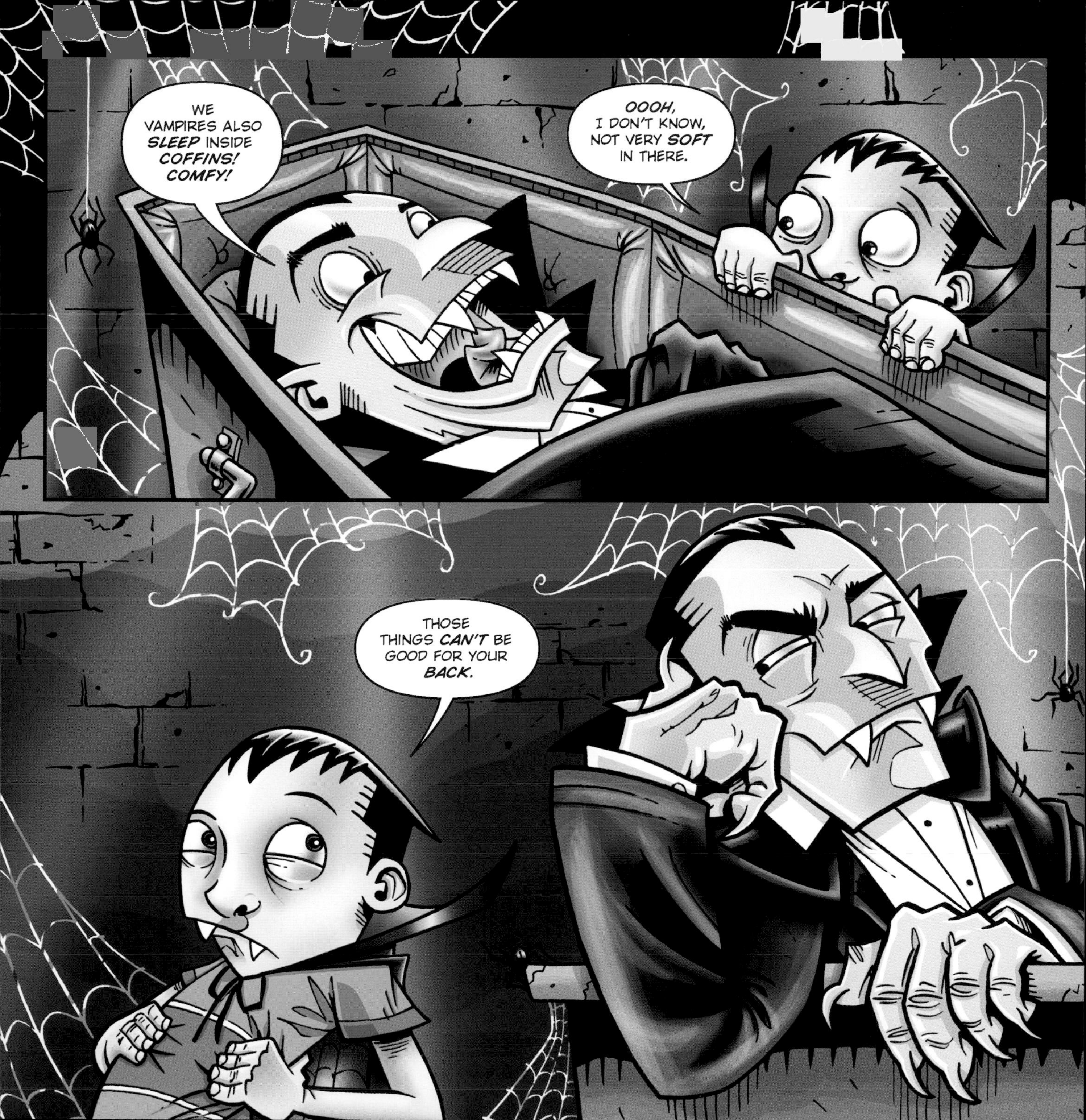
WE VAMPIRES ALSO SLEEP INSIDE COFFINS! COMFY!
OOOH, I DON'T KNOW, NOT VERY SOFT IN THERE.
THOSE THINGS CAN'T BE GOOD FOR YOUR BACK.

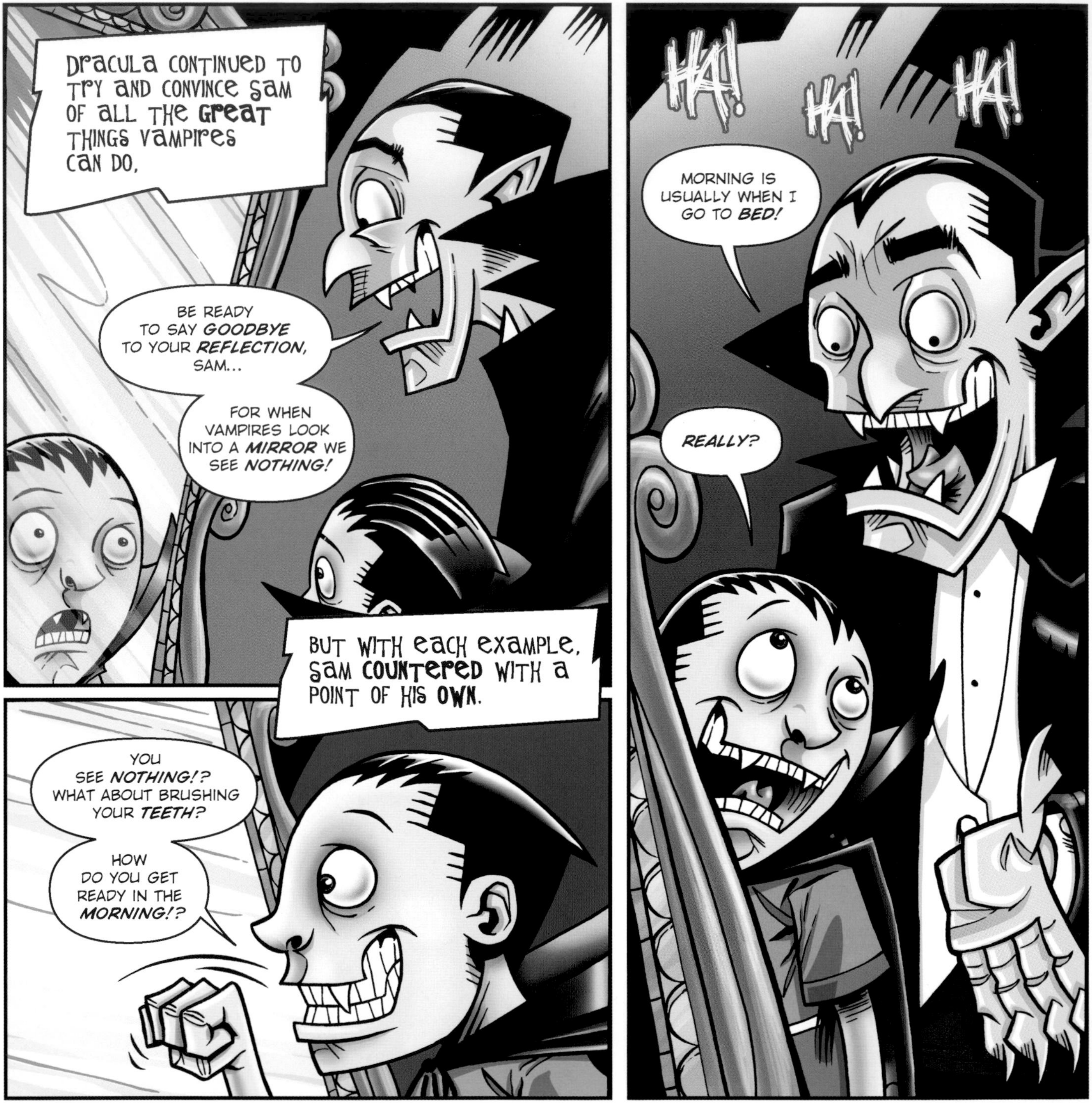

DRACULA CONTINUED TO TRY AND CONVINCE SAM OF ALL THE GREAT THINGS VAMPIRES CAN DO,
BE READY TO SAY GOODBYE TO YOUR REFLECTION, SAM...
FOR WHEN VAMPIRES LOOK INTO A MIRROR WE SEE NOTHING!
BUT WITH EACH EXAMPLE, SAM COUNTERED WITH A POINT OF HIS OWN.
YOU SEE NOTHING!? WHAT ABOUT BRUSHING YOUR TEETH?
HOW DO YOU GET READY IN THE MORNING!?
HA! HA! HA!
MORNING IS USUALLY WHEN I GO TO BED!
REALLY?

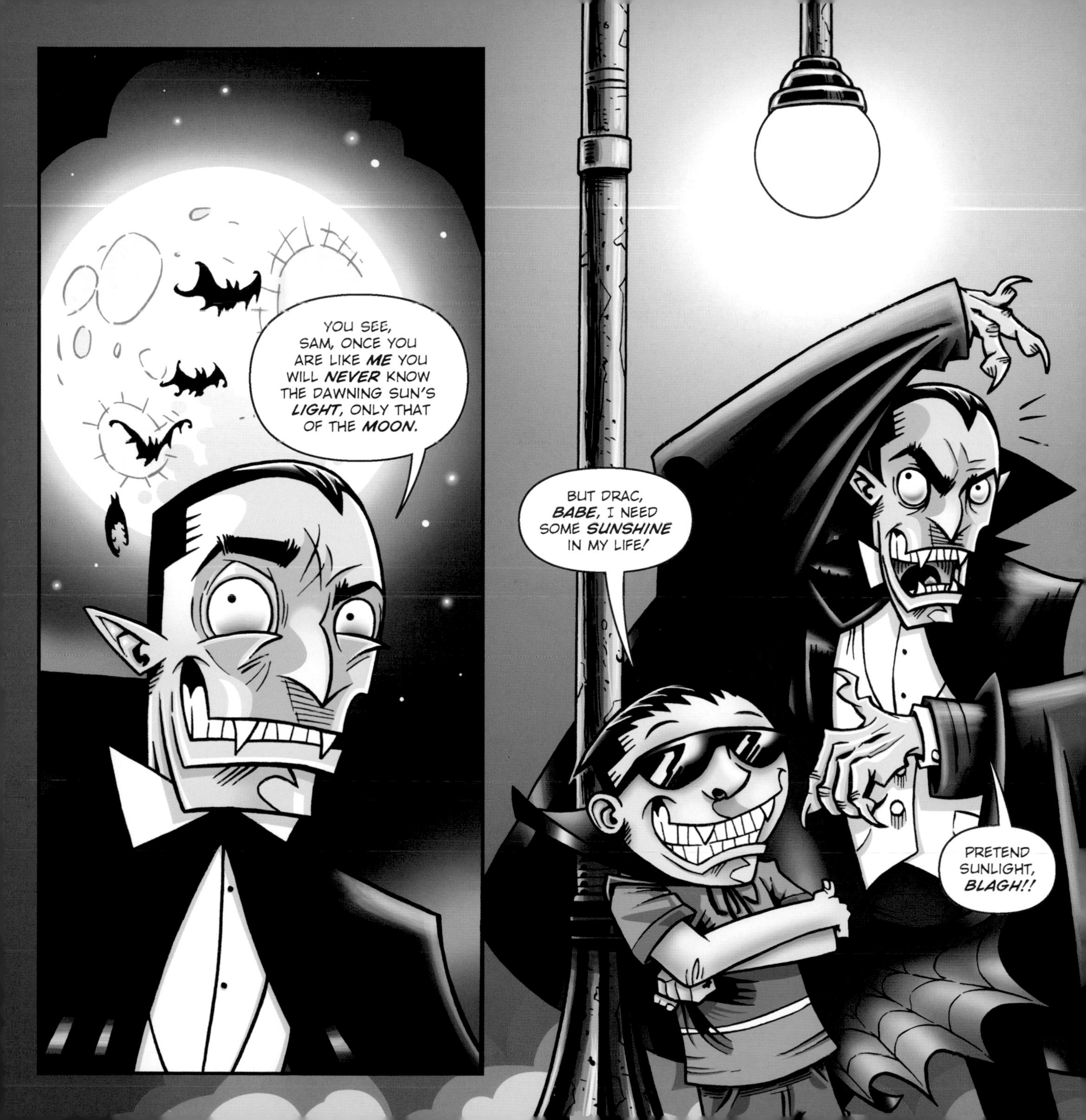
YOU SEE, SAM, ONCE YOU ARE LIKE *ME* YOU WILL *NEVER* KNOW THE DAWNING SUN'S *LIGHT*, ONLY THAT OF THE *MOON*.
BUT DRAC, *BABE*, I NEED SOME *SUNSHINE* IN MY LIFE!
PRETEND SUNLIGHT, *BLAGH!!*

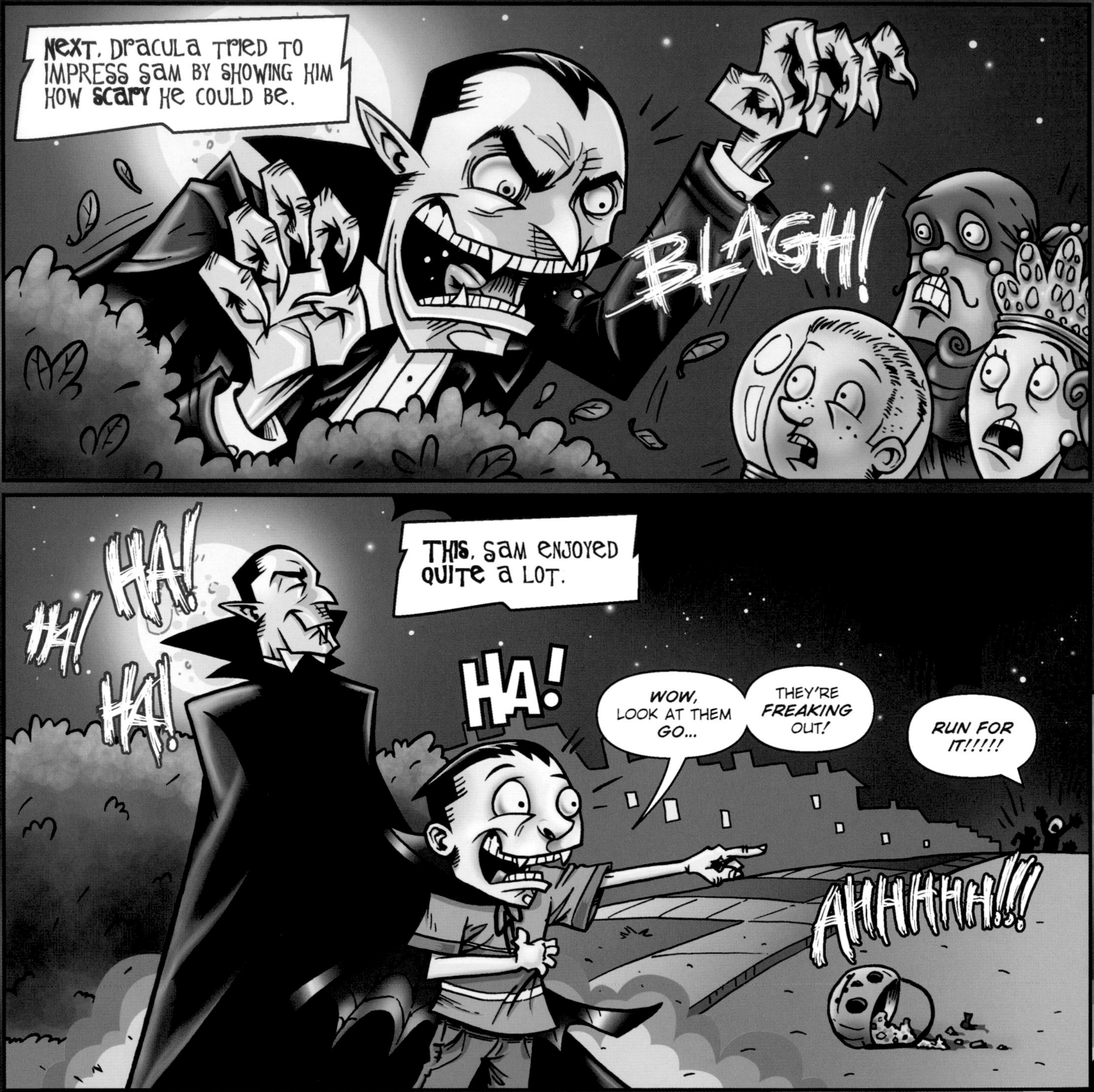
NEXT, DRACULA TRIED TO IMPRESS SAM BY SHOWING HIM HOW SCARY HE COULD BE.
BLAGH!
THIS, SAM ENJOYED QUITE A LOT.
HA! HA! HA!
HA!
WOW, LOOK AT THEM GO...
THEY'RE FREAKING OUT!
RUN FOR IT!!!!!
AHHHHH!!!

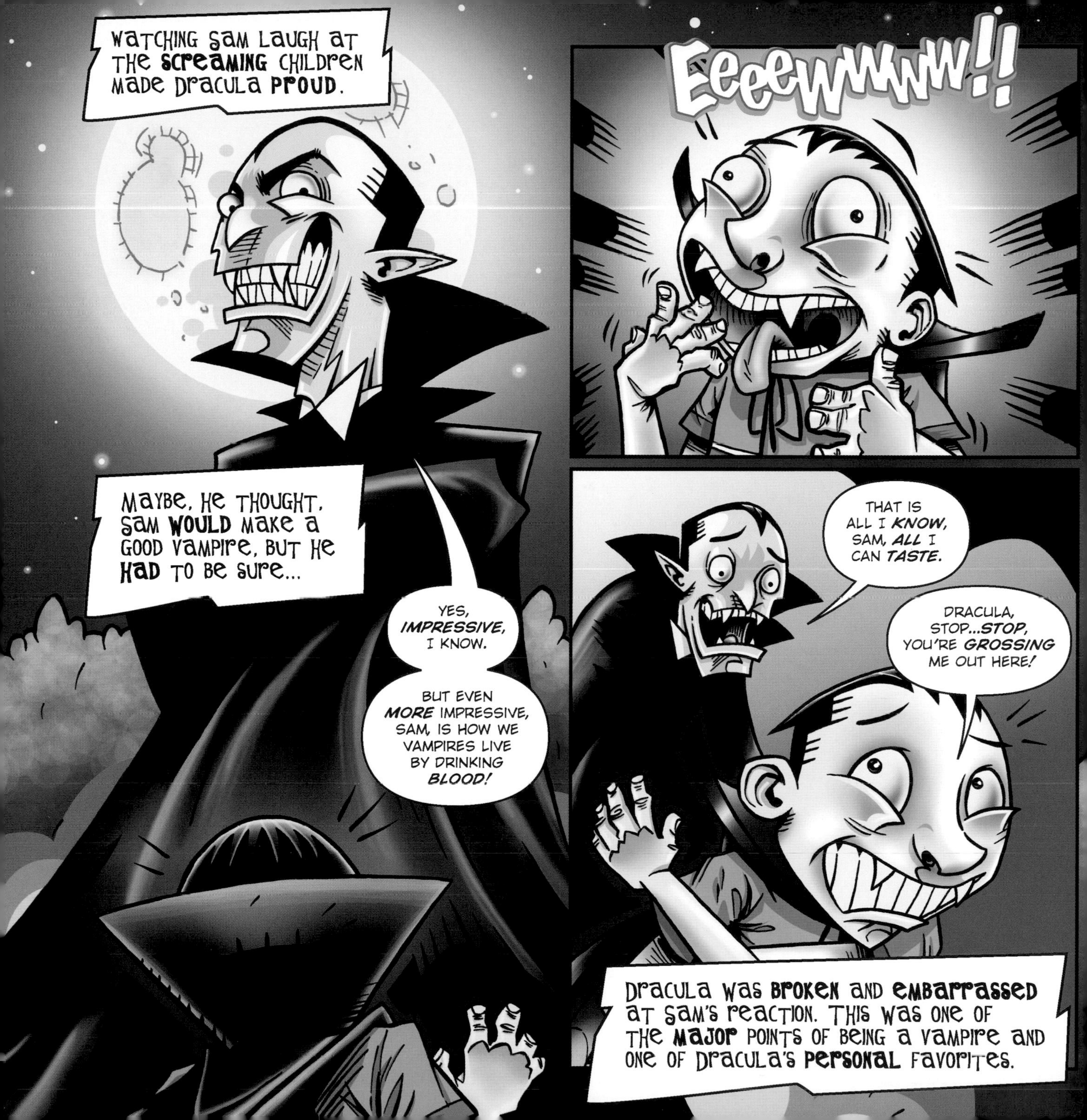
WATCHING SAM LAUGH AT THE SCREAMING CHILDREN MADE DRACULA PROUD.
EEEEWWWWW!!
MAYBE, HE THOUGHT, SAM WOULD MAKE A GOOD VAMPIRE, BUT HE HAD TO BE SURE...
YES, IMPRESSIVE, I KNOW.
BUT EVEN MORE IMPRESSIVE, SAM, IS HOW WE VAMPIRES LIVE BY DRINKING BLOOD!
THAT IS ALL I KNOW, SAM, ALL I CAN TASTE.
DRACULA, STOP...STOP, YOU'RE GROSSING ME OUT HERE!
DRACULA WAS BROKEN AND EMBARRASSED AT SAM'S REACTION. THIS WAS ONE OF THE MAJOR POINTS OF BEING A VAMPIRE AND ONE OF DRACULA'S PERSONAL FAVORITES.

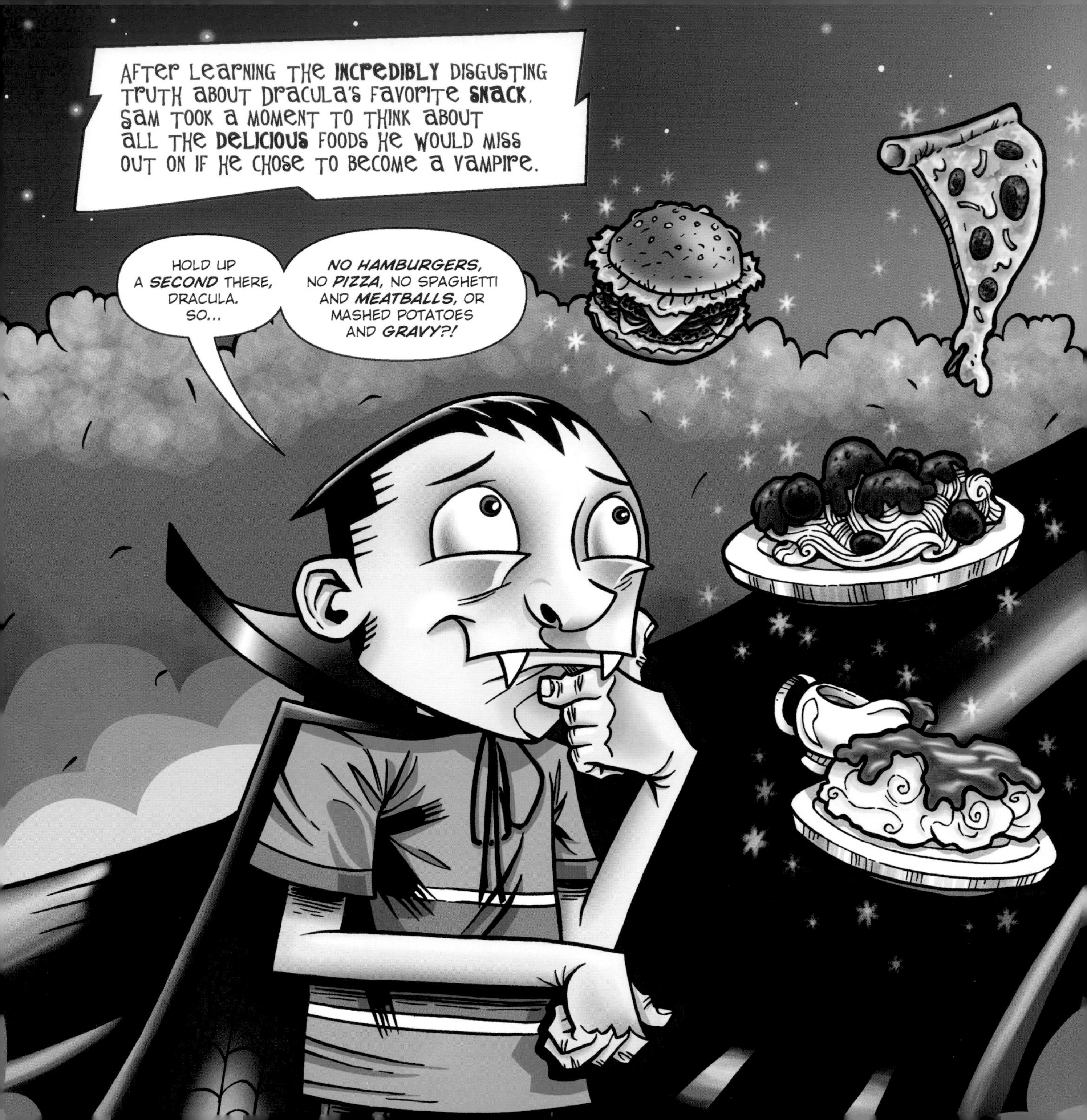
AFTER LEARNING THE INCREDIBLY DISGUSTING TRUTH ABOUT DRACULA'S FAVORITE SNACK, SAM TOOK A MOMENT TO THINK ABOUT ALL THE DELICIOUS FOODS HE WOULD MISS OUT ON IF HE CHOSE TO BECOME A VAMPIRE.
HOLD UP A SECOND THERE, DRACULA. SO...
NO HAMBURGERS, NO PIZZA, NO SPAGHETTI AND MEATBALLS, OR MASHED POTATOES AND GRAVY?!

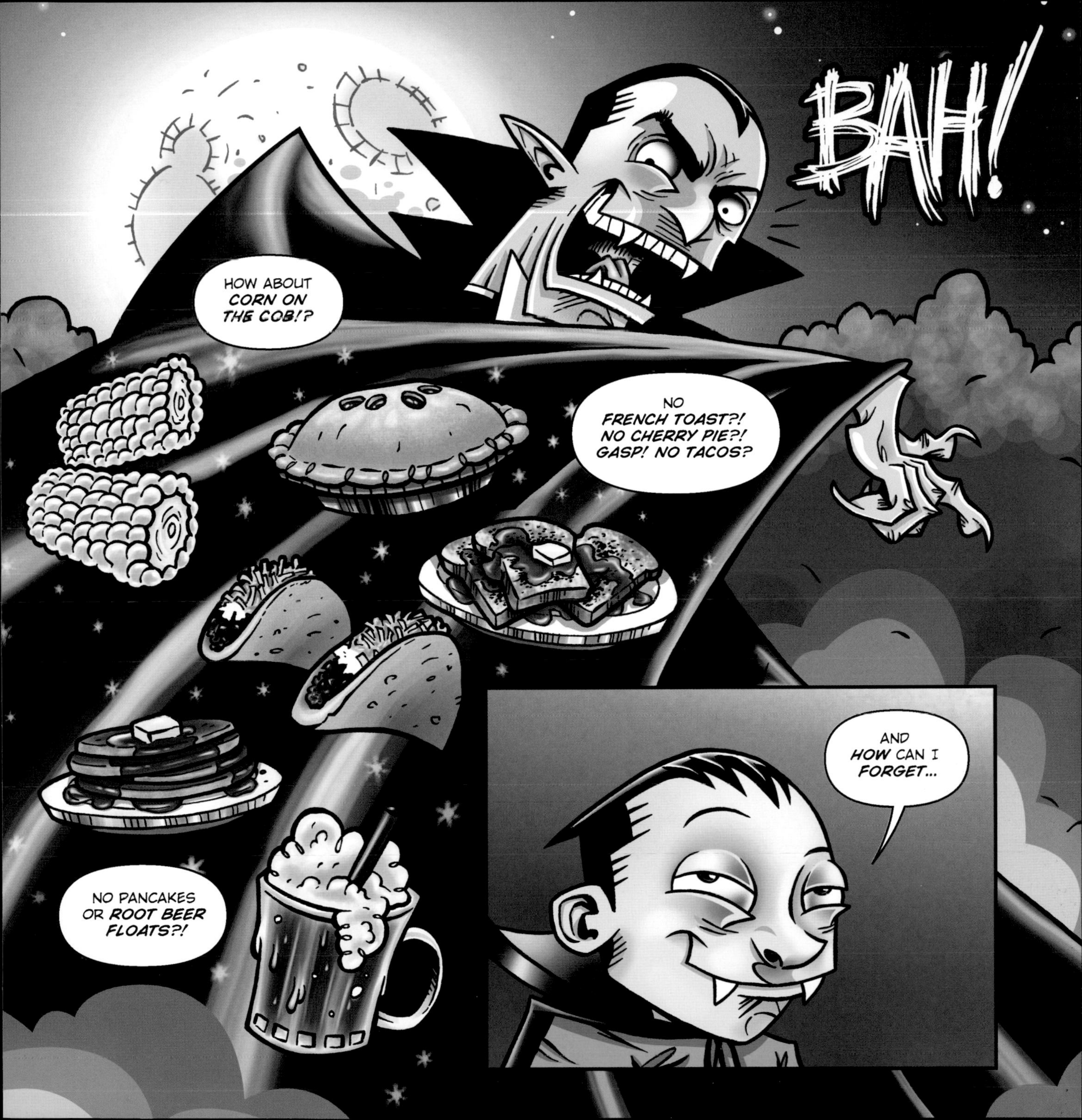
BAH!
HOW ABOUT CORN ON THE COB!?
NO FRENCH TOAST?! NO CHERRY PIE?! GASP! NO TACOS?
NO PANCAKES OR ROOT BEER FLOATS?!
AND HOW CAN I FORGET...

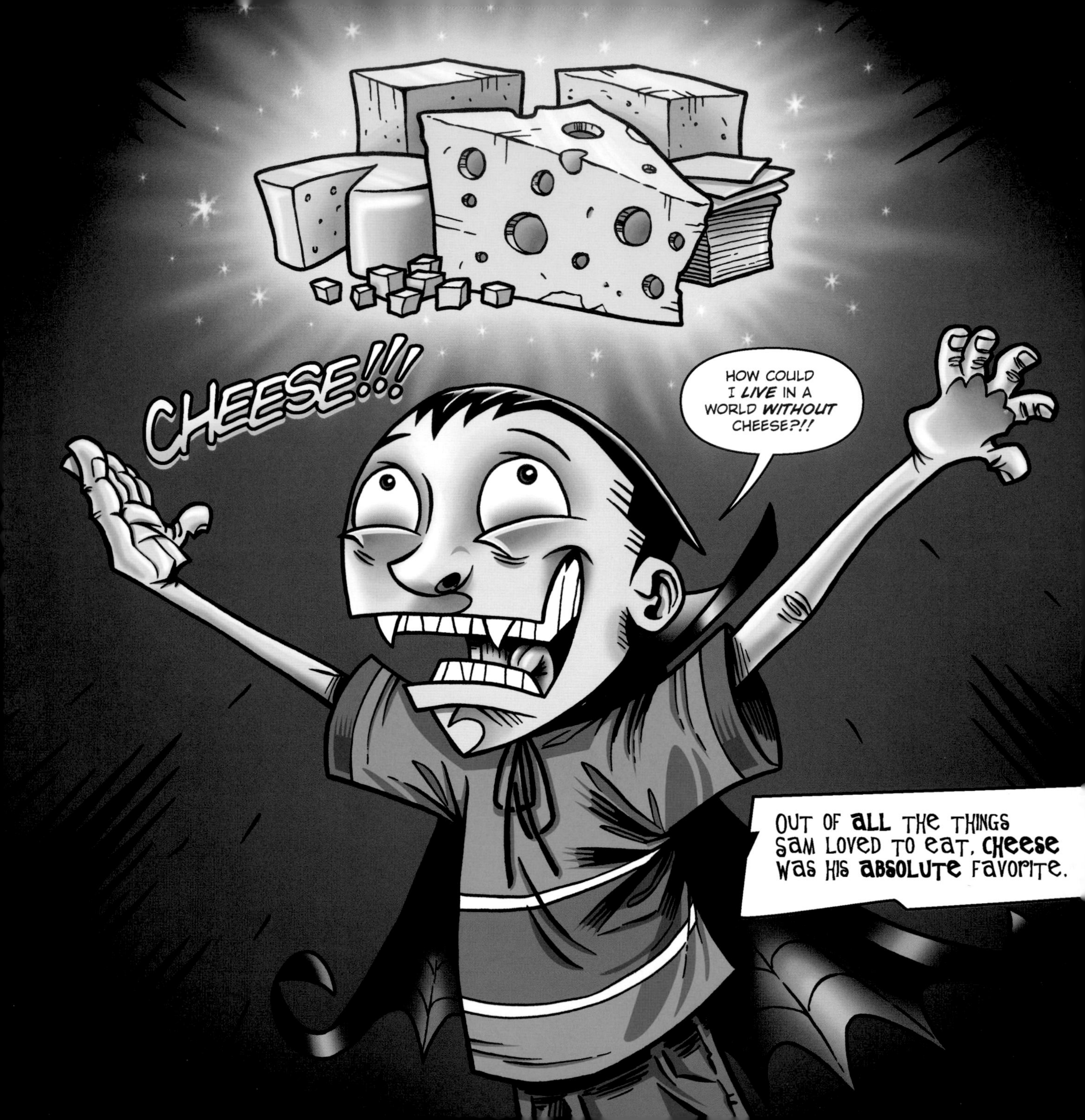
CHEESE!!!
HOW COULD I LIVE IN A WORLD WITHOUT CHEESE?!!
OUT OF ALL THE THINGS SAM LOVED TO EAT, CHEESE WAS HIS ABSOLUTE FAVORITE.

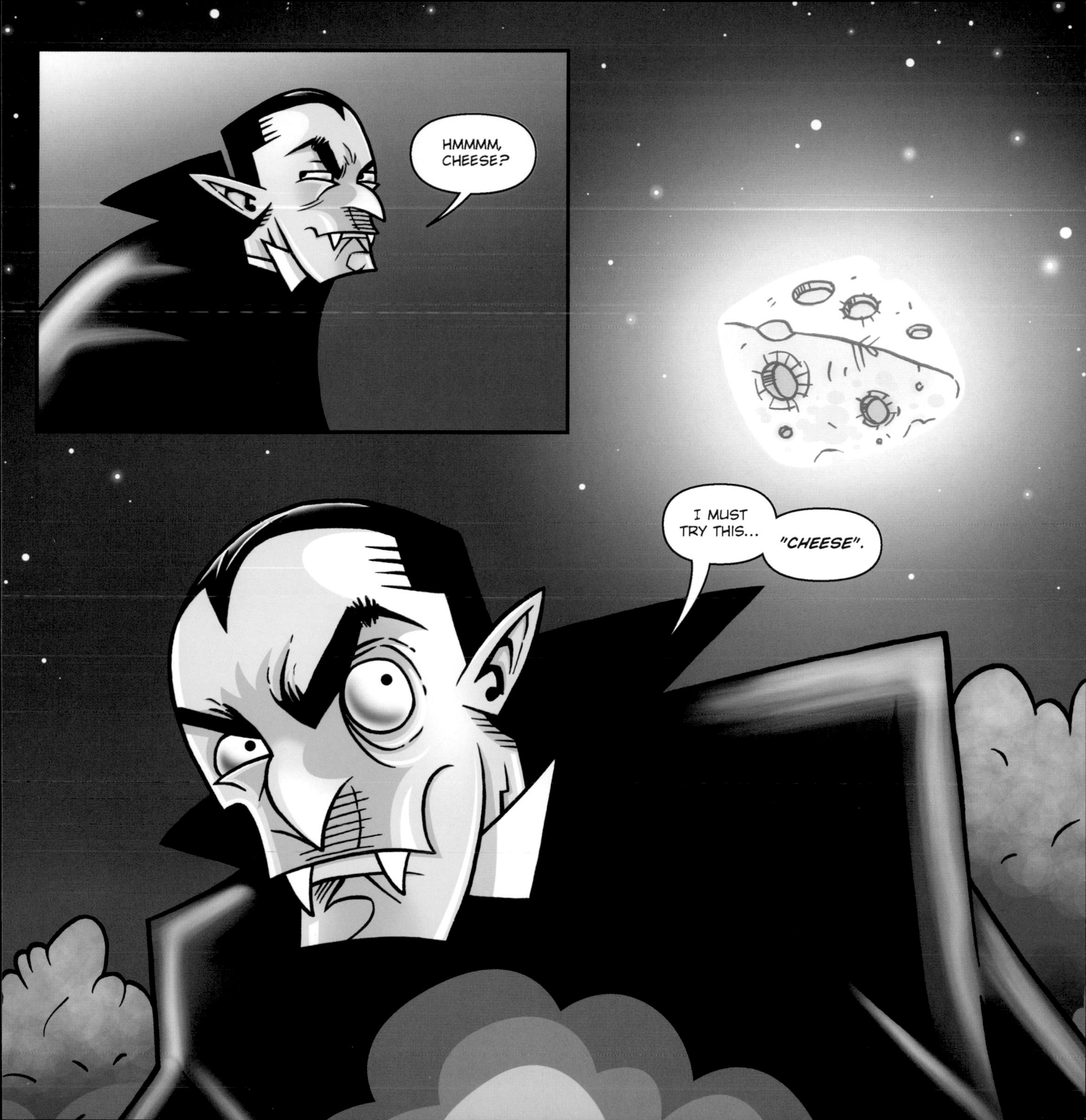
HMMMM, CHEESE?
I MUST TRY THIS...
"CHEESE".

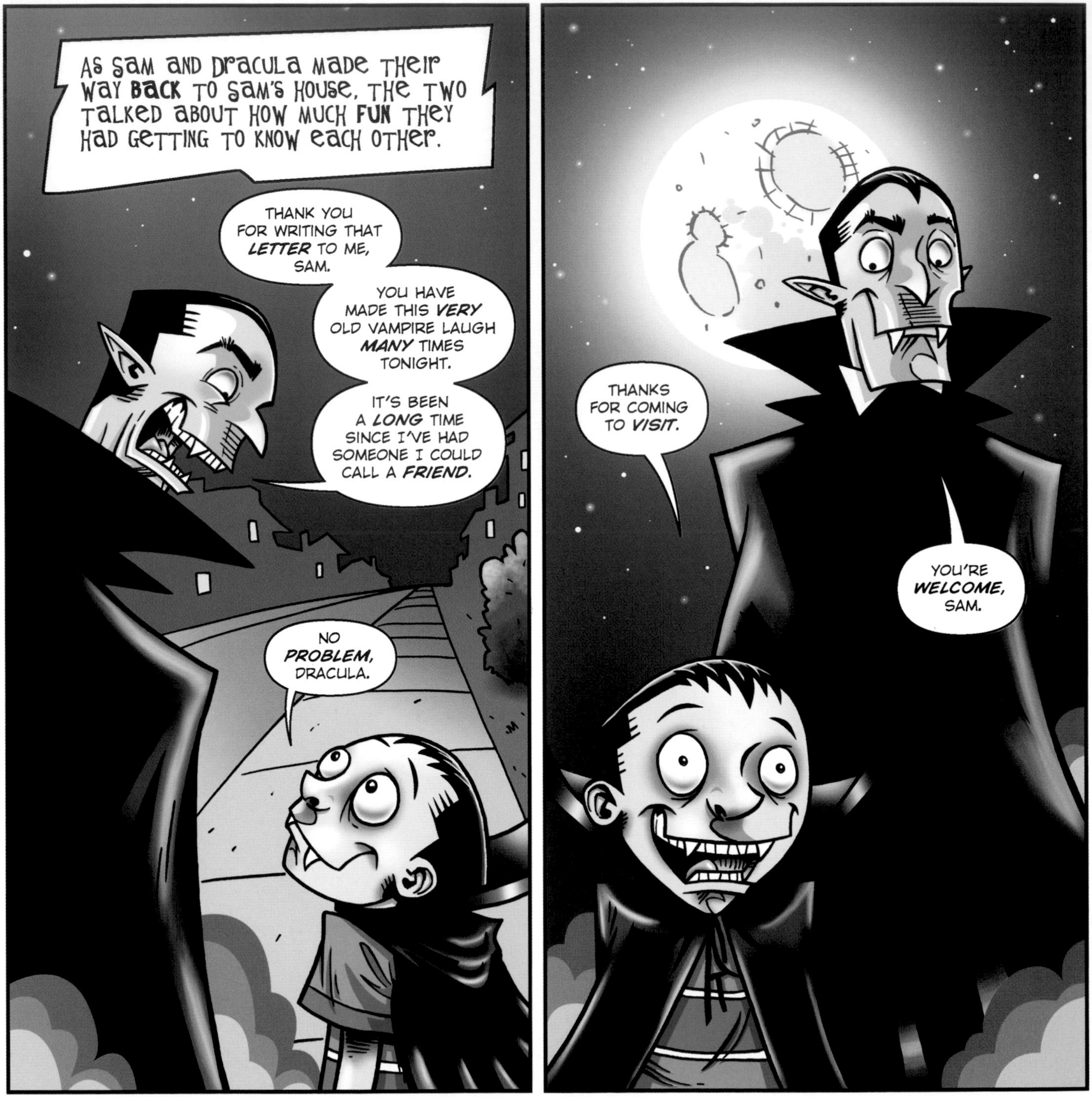
AS SAM AND DRACULA MADE THEIR WAY BACK TO SAM'S HOUSE, THE TWO TALKED ABOUT HOW MUCH FUN THEY HAD GETTING TO KNOW EACH OTHER.
THANK YOU FOR WRITING THAT LETTER TO ME, SAM.
YOU HAVE MADE THIS VERY OLD VAMPIRE LAUGH MANY TIMES TONIGHT.
IT'S BEEN A LONG TIME SINCE I'VE HAD SOMEONE I COULD CALL A FRIEND.
NO PROBLEM, DRACULA.
THANKS FOR COMING TO VISIT.
YOU'RE WELCOME, SAM.

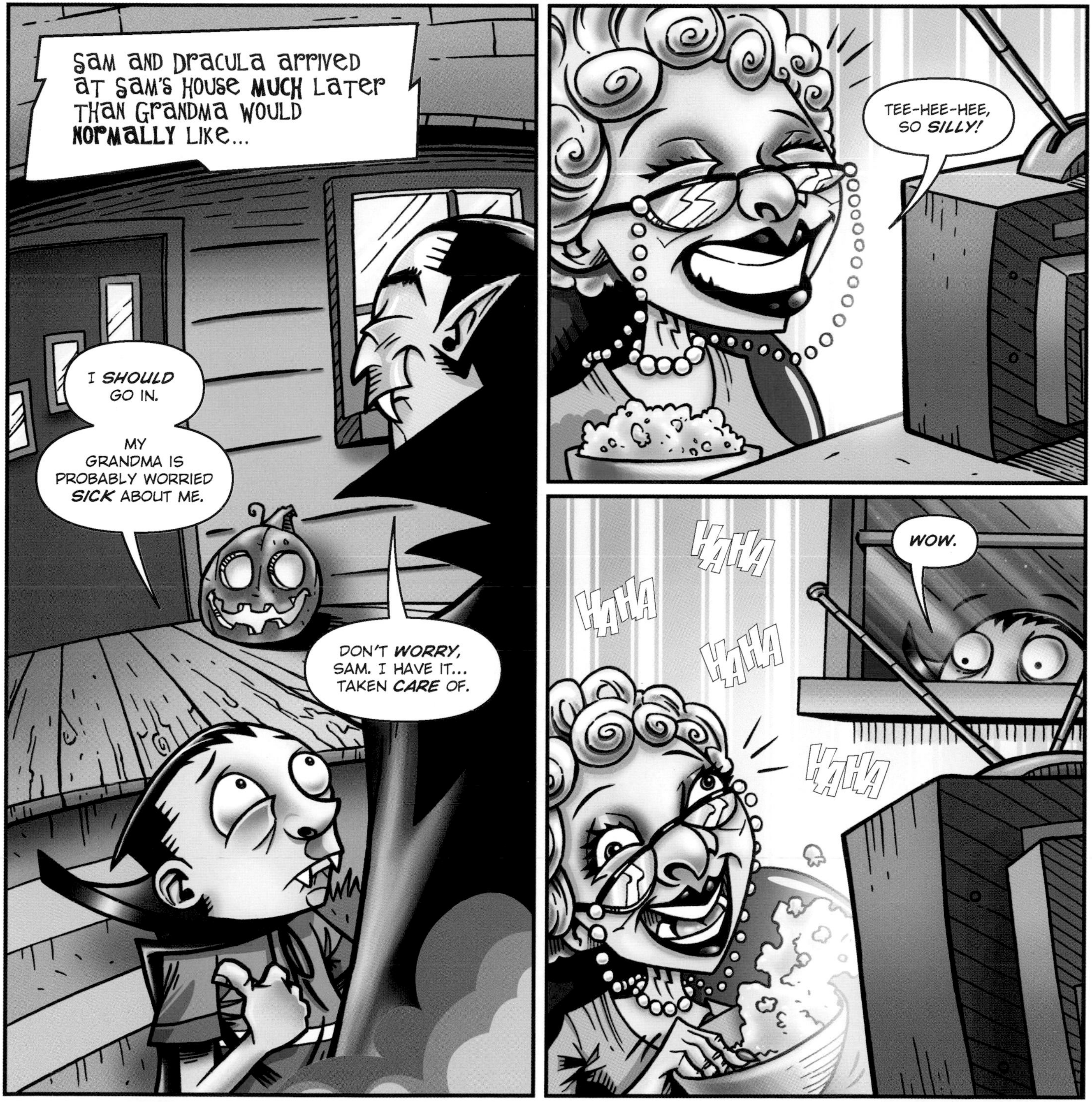
SAM AND DRACULA ARRIVED AT SAM'S HOUSE MUCH LATER THAN GRANDMA WOULD NORMALLY LIKE...
I SHOULD GO IN.
MY GRANDMA IS PROBABLY WORRIED SICK ABOUT ME.
DON'T WORRY, SAM. I HAVE IT... TAKEN CARE OF.
TEE-HEE-HEE, SO SILLY!
HAHA
HAHA
WOW.
HAHA
HAHA

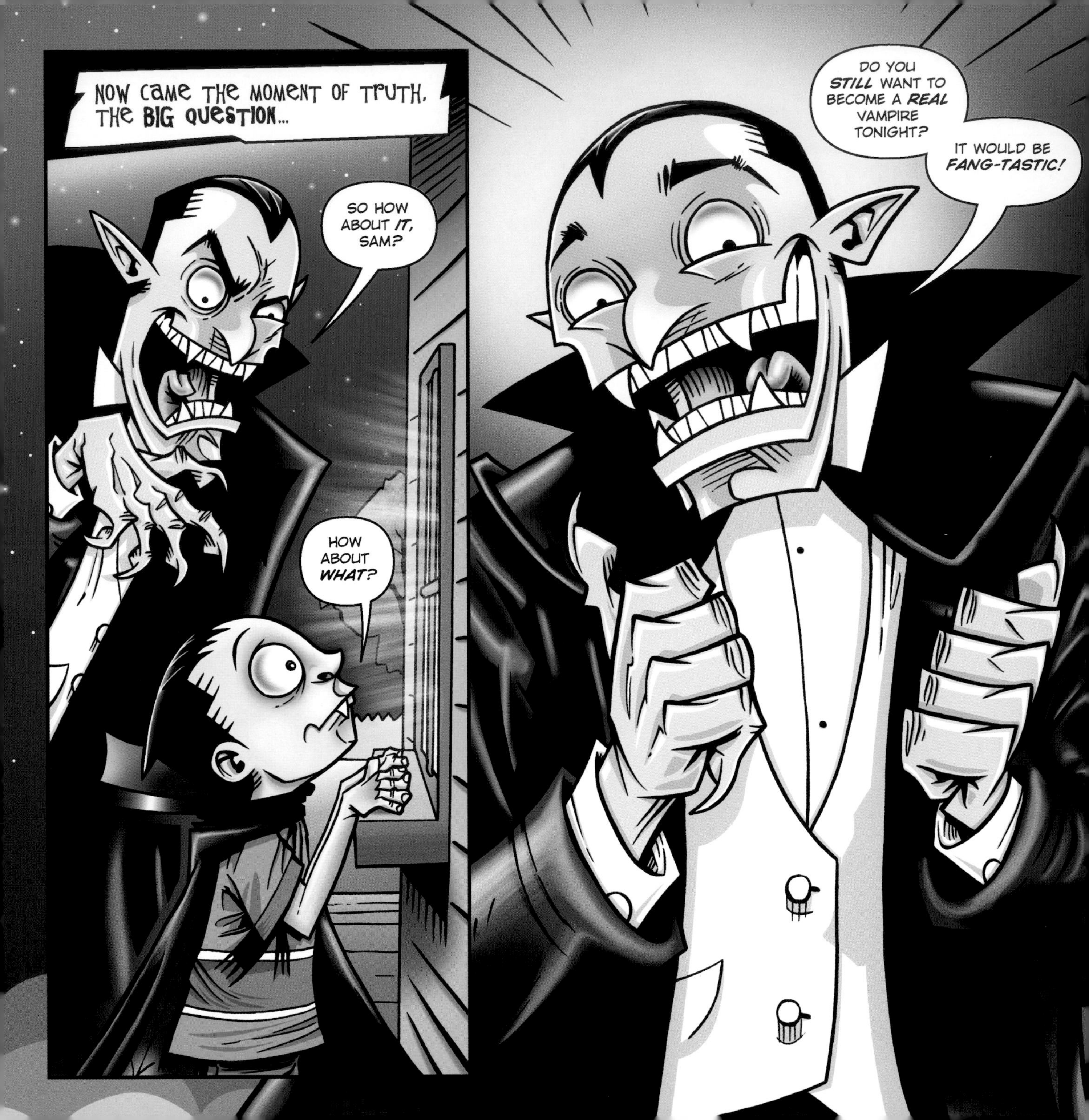
NOW CAME THE MOMENT OF TRUTH. THE BIG QUESTION...
SO HOW ABOUT IT, SAM?
HOW ABOUT WHAT?
DO YOU STILL WANT TO BECOME A REAL VAMPIRE TONIGHT?
IT WOULD BE FANG-TASTIC!

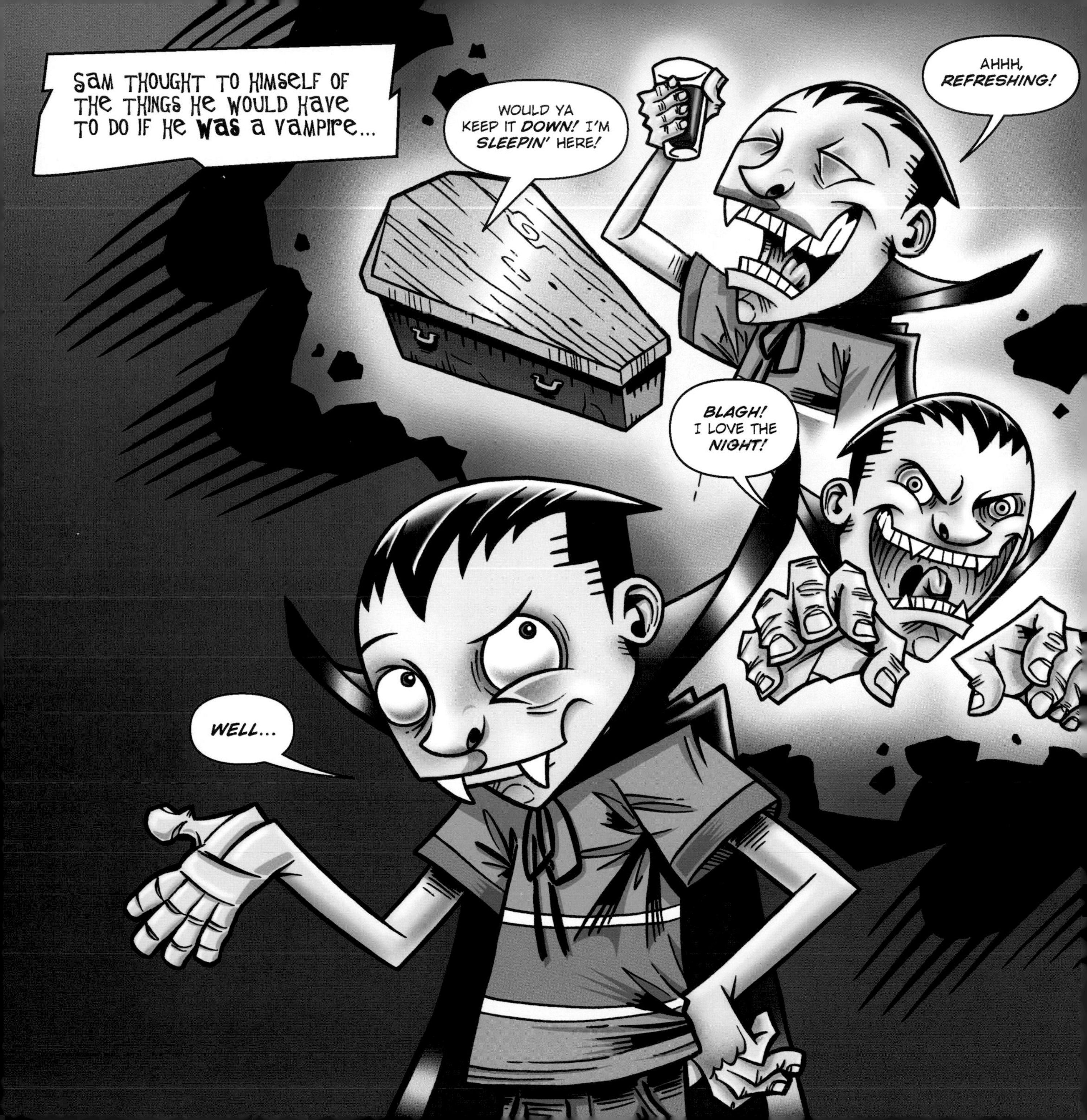
SAM THOUGHT TO HIMSELF OF THE THINGS HE WOULD HAVE TO DO IF HE **WAS** A VAMPIRE...
WOULD YA KEEP IT *DOWN!* I'M *SLEEPIN'* HERE!
AHHH, *REFRESHING!*
BLAGH! I LOVE THE *NIGHT!*
WELL...

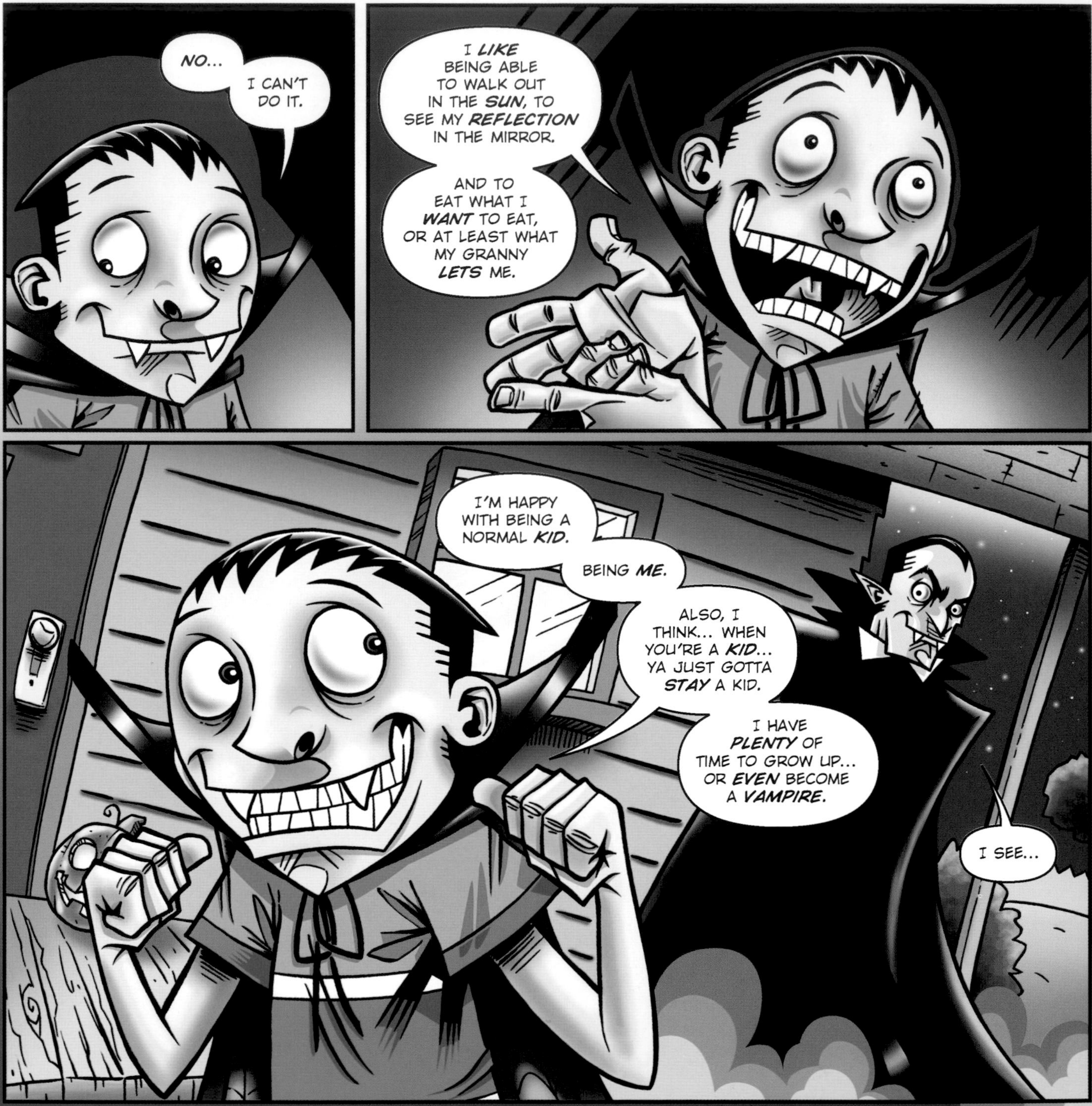
NO...
I CAN'T DO IT.
I LIKE BEING ABLE TO WALK OUT IN THE SUN, TO SEE MY REFLECTION IN THE MIRROR.
AND TO EAT WHAT I WANT TO EAT, OR AT LEAST WHAT MY GRANNY LETS ME.
I'M HAPPY WITH BEING A NORMAL KID.
BEING ME.
ALSO, I THINK... WHEN YOU'RE A KID... YA JUST GOTTA STAY A KID.
I HAVE PLENTY OF TIME TO GROW UP... OR EVEN BECOME A VAMPIRE.
I SEE...

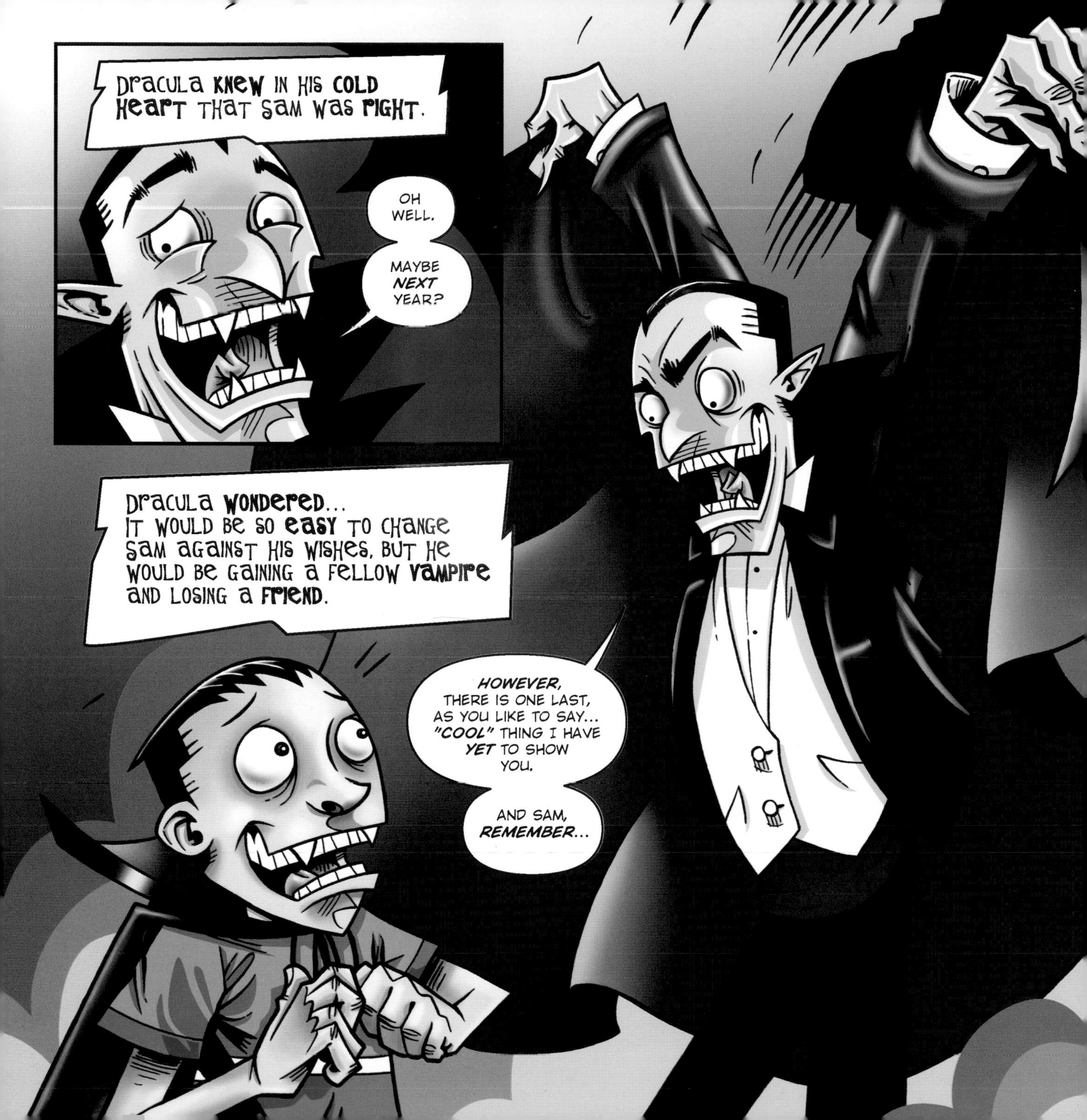
DRACULA KNEW IN HIS COLD HEART THAT SAM WAS RIGHT.
OH WELL.
MAYBE NEXT YEAR?
DRACULA WONDERED... IT WOULD BE SO EASY TO CHANGE SAM AGAINST HIS WISHES, BUT HE WOULD BE GAINING A FELLOW VAMPIRE AND LOSING A FRIEND.
HOWEVER, THERE IS ONE LAST, AS YOU LIKE TO SAY... "COOL" THING I HAVE YET TO SHOW YOU.
AND SAM, REMEMBER...

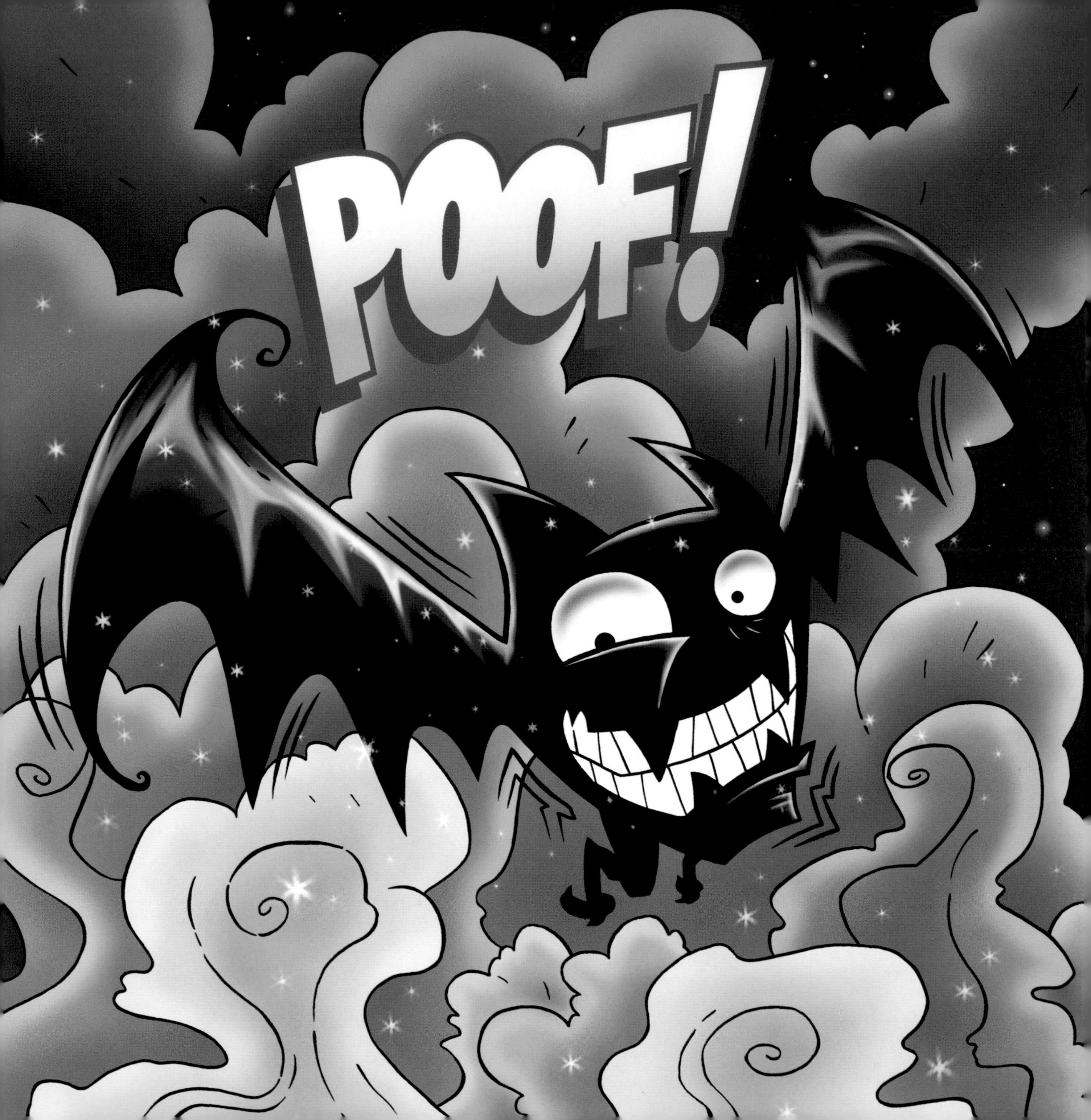
POOF!

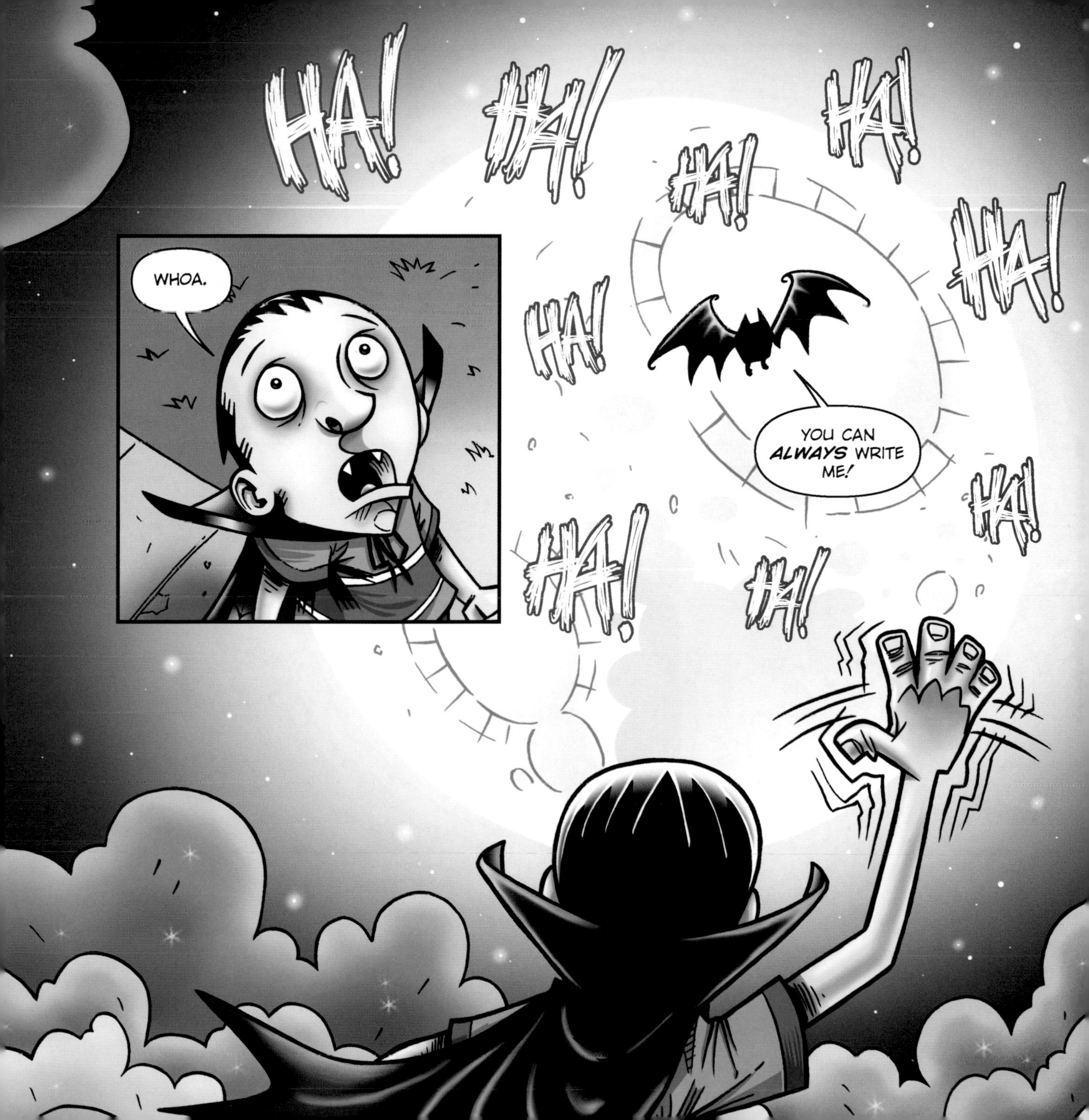
HA!
HA!
HA!
HA!
HA!
WHOA.
HA!
YOU CAN ALWAYS WRITE ME!
HA!
HA!
HA!

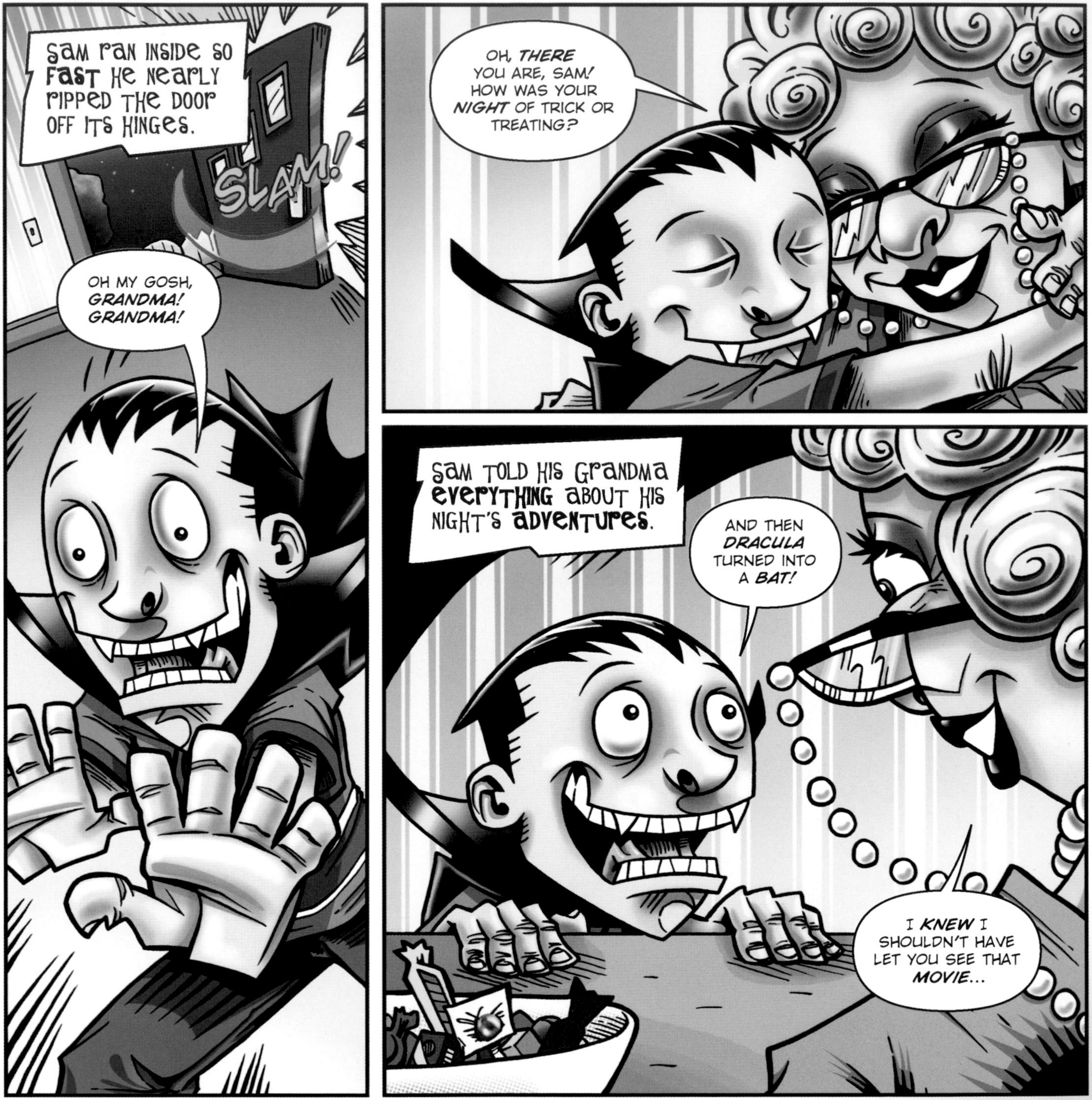
SAM RAN INSIDE SO FAST HE NEARLY RIPPED THE DOOR OFF ITS HINGES.
SLAM!
OH MY GOSH, GRANDMA! GRANDMA!
OH, THERE YOU ARE, SAM! HOW WAS YOUR NIGHT OF TRICK OR TREATING?
SAM TOLD HIS GRANDMA EVERYTHING ABOUT HIS NIGHT'S ADVENTURES.
AND THEN DRACULA TURNED INTO A BAT!
I KNEW I SHOULDN'T HAVE LET YOU SEE THAT MOVIE...

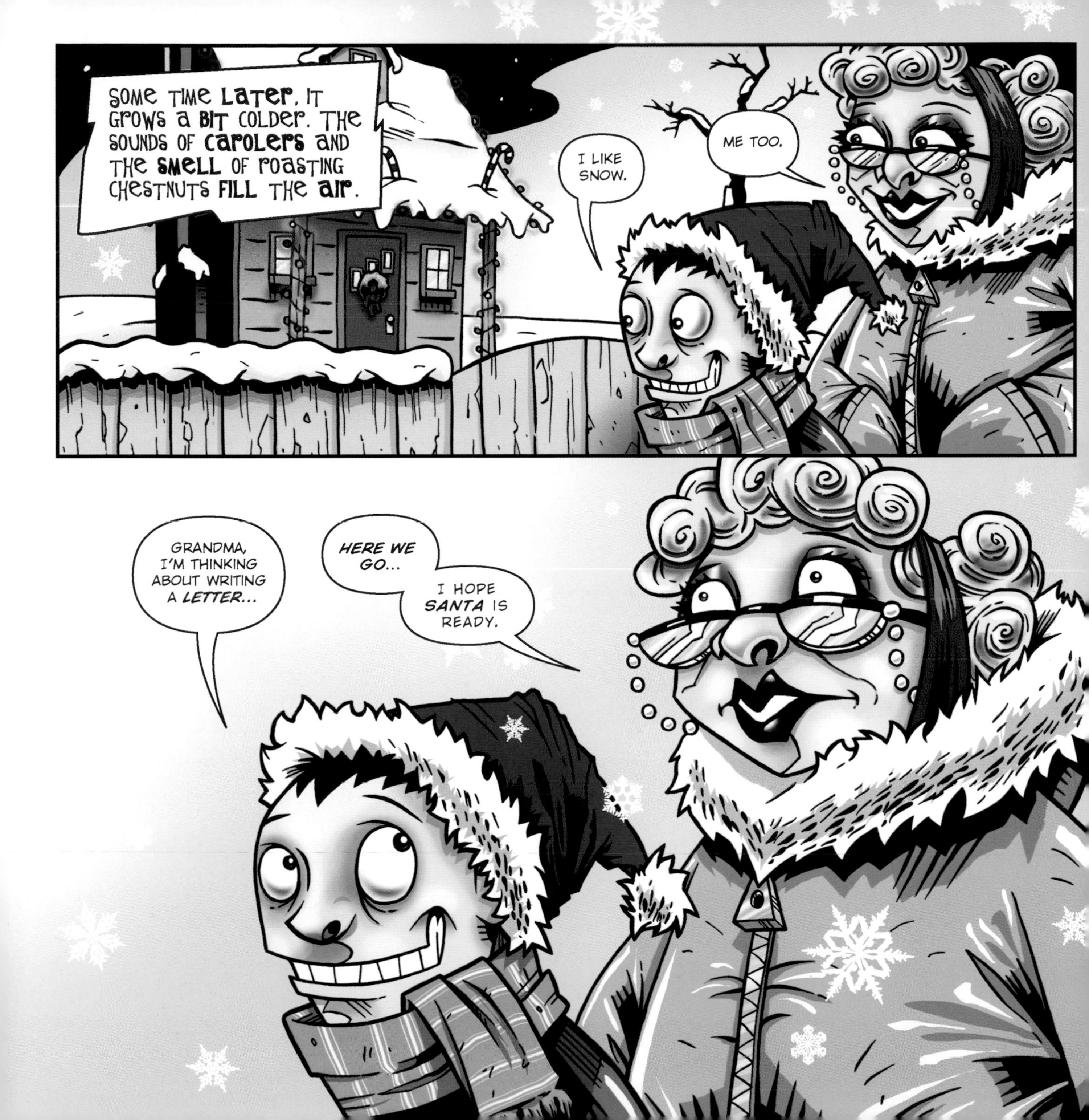
SOME TIME LATER, IT GROWS A BIT COLDER. THE SOUNDS OF CAROLERS AND THE SMELL OF ROASTING CHESTNUTS FILL THE AIR.
I LIKE SNOW.
ME TOO.
GRANDMA, I'M THINKING ABOUT WRITING A LETTER...
HERE WE GO...
I HOPE SANTA IS READY.

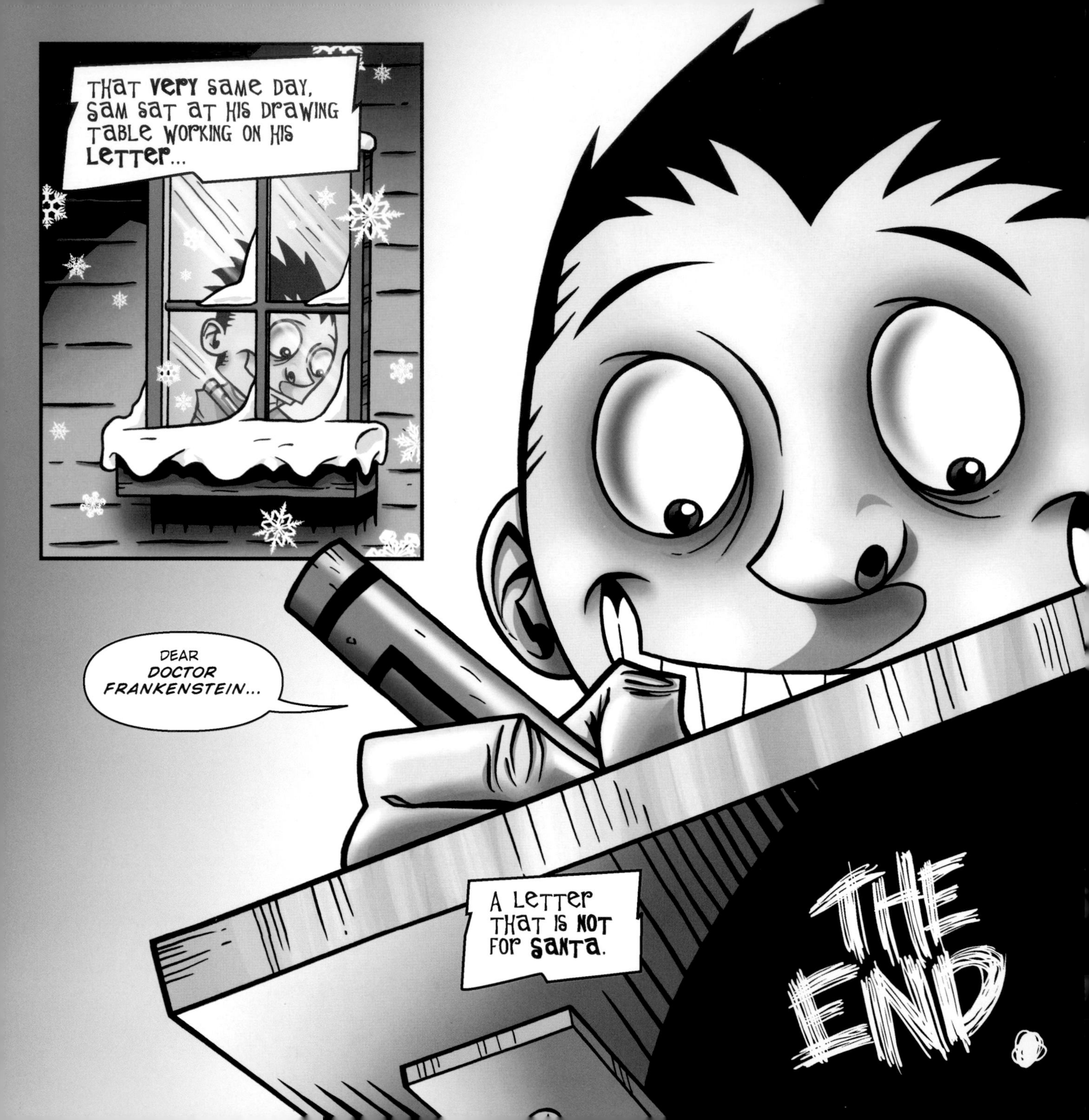
THAT VERY SAME DAY, SAM SAT AT HIS DRAWING TABLE WORKING ON HIS LETTER...
DEAR DOCTOR FRANKENSTEIN...
A LETTER THAT IS NOT FOR SANTA.
THE END.

I WOULD LIKE TO THANK MY FAMILY AND FRIENDS FOR SUPPORTING ME AND LETTING ME TELL MY CRAZY STORIES. I'D LIKE TO GIVE SPECIAL THANKS TO DANIELLE FOR PUTTING UP WITH THE LONG SLEEPLESS NIGHTS AND MY "WORK WEEKENDS" THAT NEVER SEEMED TO END.

OH AND, THANKS TO VINNY, MY CLOSEST FRIEND, AND THE GUY THAT MADE THIS BOOK HAPPEN.

--JOSH

I'D LIKE TO THANK MY FAMILY AND FRIENDS, IT'S NOT EASY MAKING THESE DARN BOOKS, BUT WITH ALL OF YOU IN MY LIFE IT'S NOT AS HARD.

YOU'RE WELCOME JOSH, AND THANK YOU.

A **BIG TIME** THANKS TO MY MOM AND POPS.

--VINNY

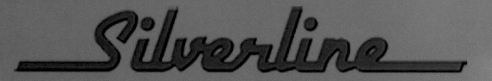

Silverline

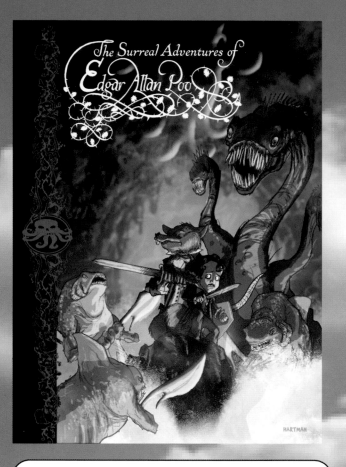

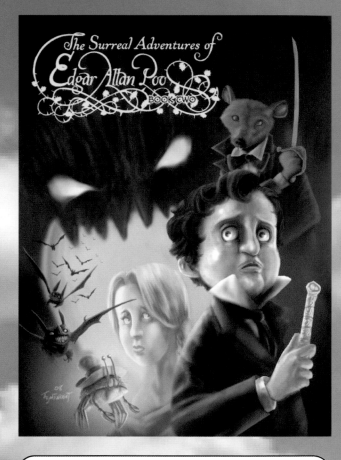

The Surreal Adventures of
Edgar Allan Poo
HARTMAN

The Surreal Adventures of Edgar Allan Poo
by Dwight L. MacPherson and Thomas Boatwright

Edgar Allan Poe just lost everything. His dead wife is haunting him in his dreams, his latest book has bombed, and the imaginationthat fueled his stories is gone. His prayer to never dream againis answered one evening when he falls asleep in an outhouse.His discarded creativity takes the form of his dream child, EdgarAllan Poo, who must now undergo a strange odyssey through the poet's troubled mind.

96 PAGES SC FC $9.99 8.5" x 11" ISBN: 978-1-58240-816-3

The Surreal Adventures of
Edgar Allan Poo
BOOK TWO

The Surreal Adventures of Edgar Allan Poo Book Two
by Dwight L. MacPherson and Avery Butterworth

It's a clash of the titans as the forces of the Nightmare King collide with the armies of Terra Somnium in a battle to determine the fate of the Dream Child! In the end, Edgar Allan Poo must stand alone to rescue his mother and prevent the dark lord from trapping him in the realm of dreams...forever!

96 PAGES SC FC $12.99 8.5" x 11" ISBN: 978-1-58240-975-7

...BECAUSE EVERY CLOUD HAS ONE

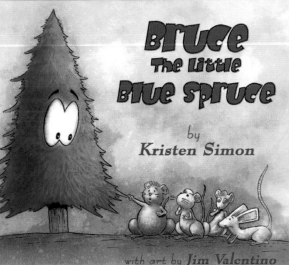

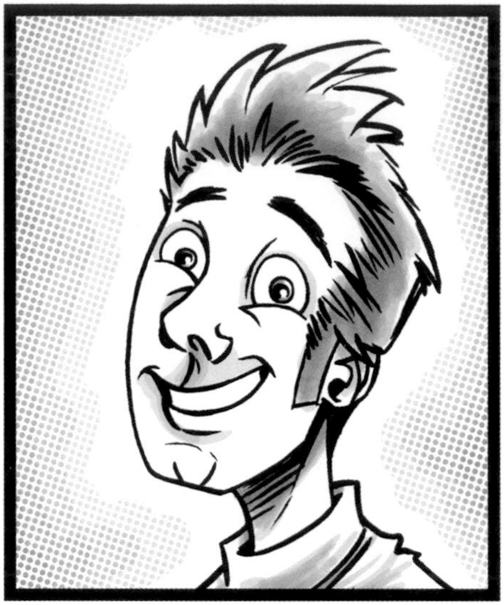

JOSH

JOSHUA WILLIAMSON HAS WANTED TO WRITE COMICS SINCE HE WAS A LITTLE KID, AND HAS BEEN SELF PUBLISHING BOOKS SINCE 2001. HE HAS WORKED IN NEARLY EVERY STAGE OF THE COMIC CREATION PROCESS: LETTERING, COLORING AND EVEN HAND FEEDING A PRINTER TO MAKE SURE HE COULD FINISH A MINI-COMIC IN TIME FOR A CONVENTION.

AFTER LIVING IN SOUTHERN CALIFORNIA HIS WHOLE LIFE, HE RECENTLY MOVED TO PORTLAND, OREGON WHERE THE WEATHER IS PERFECT FOR STAYING INDOORS WRITING ALL DAY AND SLEEPING IN.

WHEN JOSH ISN'T BUSY WRITING OR TRYING TO HITCH RIDES FROM AN AIRPORT HE LIKES TO GO KAYAKING WITH HIS BUDS, WATCH TV SHOWS ON DVD AND HANG WITH HIS FIANCÉ, DANIELLE, AND HIS SMALL DOG, CORDELIA.

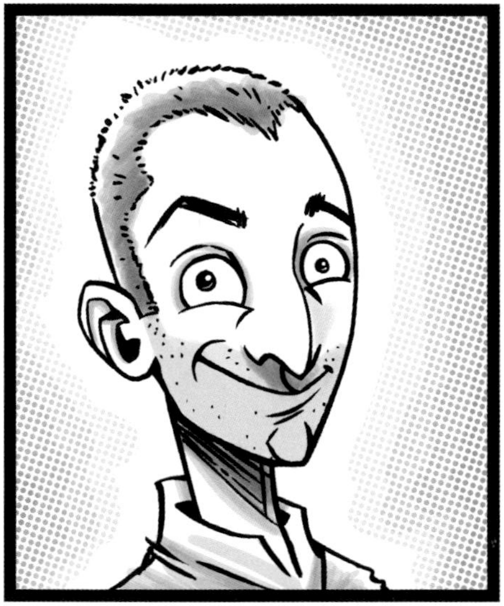

VINNY

VICEANTE "VINNY" NAVARRETE HAS BEEN DRAWING AND MAKING THINGS SINCE HE WAS FIVE YEARS OLD. SOME OF HIS EARLY CREATIVE INFLUENCES INCLUDE: SESAME STREET, READING RAINBOW, HE-MAN, AND THE TEENAGE MUTANT NINJA TURTLES.

BEFORE "DEAR DRACULA", VINNY WAS SELF PUBLISHING AND WORKING FREE LANCE, WITH PROJECTS RANGING FROM LOGO AND CHARACTER DESIGN TO MURAL PAINTING.

WHEN HE'S NOT PENCILING, INKING, OR COLORING ON A PROJECT, VINNY LOVES TO SHOOT HOOPS. LEGEND HAS IT, HE ONCE BAILED ON SOME FRIENDS WHO NEEDED A RIDE FROM THE AIRPORT TO GO PLAY BALL.

VINNY RESIDES IN OREGON, WHICH (BY THE WAY) IS "BEAUTIFUL COUNTRY".